Taking Doreen out of the Sky

'Alan Beard's stories belong to a Birmingham tradition of gritty realism that goes back to the work of Walter Allen, John Hampson and Leslie Halward in the 'thirties. Here is the life that goes on in today's factories, pubs and council flats, observed with humour, compassion and an eye for the telling detail'

David Lodge

'It was quite evident from the first story we printed, "Taking Doreen out of the Sky", that Alan Beard was a writer of real talent and originality'

Alan Ross, *London Magazine*

'Alan Beard's stories are so strong because they are full of a potent understatement. He uses deliberately downbeat, low-key effects to get at the pathos of ordinary but extra-ordinary lives. Wistfulness, nostalgia, sadness and comedy blend to give his stories that true cutting edge'

John Murray, *Panurge*

ABOUT THE AUTHOR

Alan Beard's stories have been broadcast on Radio 4 and appeared in numerous magazines including *London Magazine, Panurge, Critical Quarterly* and *Malahat Review.* His work has been in several anthologies including *Best Short Stories 1991* (Heinemann) and *Telling Stories Volume 3* (Sceptre). He won the Tom-Gallon Award in 1989. Married with two children, he has lived and worked in Birmingham since 1982.

ABOUT TINDAL STREET FICTION GROUP

TSFG is a discussion, reading and support group of Birmingham fiction writers founded in 1983 by Alan Mahar. With a maximum membership of twelve (six women, six men), the group meets once a fortnight at a school in Tindal Street, Balsall Heath. Most members have had stories widely published in magazines and anthologies; one has had a short story collection published; another, two novels, with a third out soon. TSFG has produced four anthologies; *Mouth: Stories from Tindal Street*, 1996, was shortlisted for the Arts Council's Raymond Williams Prize, 1997.

Taking Doreen out of the Sky

Alan Beard

Tindal Street Fiction Group

Published in 1997 by Tindal Street Fiction Group
32 Frederick Road, Birmingham B15 1JN

A CIP catalogue record for this book is available from the British Library

ISBN 0 9528246 1 2

Printed and bound in Great Britain by
Biddles Ltd, Woodbridge Park, Guildford

'Saturday in the 'Sac' was broadcast on Radio 4 in 1993 and appeared in *Malahat Review* 106, 1994, and in *Telling Stories* Vol. 3, Sceptre 1994; 'Come See About Me' appeared in *Panurge* 13, 1990, in *Best Short Stories 1991*, Heinemann, and in *The Minerva Book of Short Stories 4*, 1992; 'Betty and Brian' appeared in *Sunk Island Review* 5, 1992; 'King' appeared in *Critical Quarterly* 33 (3), 1991 (under the title 'Circle'); 'Taking Doreen out of the Sky' appeared in *London Magazine* 25 (8), 1985, and in *The View from Tindal Street: Nine Birmingham Stories*, 1986, and won the Society of Author's Tom-Gallon Award for best short story, 1988; 'Nothing Personal' appeared in *Panurge* 15/16, 1992; 'Country Life' appeared in *London Magazine* 32 (5), 1992; an earlier version of 'Why I'm Late In' appeared in *Nutshell* 12, 1990; 'Previous Lives' appeared in *London Magazine* 27 (9), 1987/8; 'A Man' appeared in *Bête Noire* 8/9, 1989; 'Dad, Mum, Paula and Tom' was broadcast on Radio 4 in 1996 and is to appear in *Sunk Island Review* 11, 1997.

To Clare, Chloe and Grace

Acknowledgements

I would like to thank all past and present members of Tindal Street Fiction Group for their support over the years and particularly Penny Rendall, Alan Mahar, Joel Lane and Julia Bell for their hard work on this book. Also for their encouragement and endorsements Matthew Gidley, Jim Crace, West Midlands Arts, Alan Ross, David Almond, John Murray and David Lodge.

Contents

Saturday in the 'Sac

This Saturday is different from the start: when we come to there's no Phillip Schofield going on downstairs and no stream of hot water being used, no yells, no music, no arguments.

'The kids are out,' I say to Denise. 'How about coffee in bed?' I don't say breakfast, neither of us eat it. Coffee and a fag. 'I'll bring an ashtray up.'

'The shopping,' she calls. 'We've done it,' I shout from the stairs. Housework, gardening, fixing the bathroom, shovelling the catshit from our entry. Always something, but she's saying yes more these days and when I get back her face is warm from sleep still. We sit there legs out in front of us talking of our childhoods. I spent mine here in 'Oxford Place, Cul-de-Sac' – I say it like I used to as a child, when I'd reel off the full address, ending with 'the Universe'. Dee's was spent a mile or two away. Two weekend sounds recall her childhood: the bells of three churches competing, and the Saturday market at six p.m. – the stacking of scaffolding, tarpaulin into the backs of vans. We haven't done this for so long, chatted like this, all kids and favourite TV programmes you can't miss, so I'm wondering how it will turn out. I can feel her soften with nostalgia as we talk and I reach out from our pasts to her breast and she moves so my hand slips further and further down.

So Saturday begins. There's nothing on this weekend besides a trip to Denise's mother, Sunday. The pull-out table and place mats with old cars on them. The homemade pineapple cake for afters which I will say is 'delilish-us', a word stumble I made twenty-odd years ago at my first meal in that house. The kids bored. Her dad and I might slip out to the pub, walking through streets still full of bells. But Saturday looks like gardening, sunbathing – hopefully – with a can or two, checking the pools. Later a film with – how do you pronounce it? – Cherie Lunghi in it. When the kids do return noisy as ever we are up singing 'She was just seventeen, you know what I mean', but soon TV, music upstairs and Louise's friends coming by drive me out into the garden. The usual Saturday in the weak sun or else real cold that passes for summer. The usual: cutting brambles, considering how Dee's warm bra-marked flesh would feel through the creased pair of gardening gloves and wondering whether she would object to me finding out. Gagging as I shovel up catshit and bury it while the sun slips higher and burns away cloud. Leaning on the fence talking to Brian, he still wearing an anorak with 'Fat Willy' on the back. He's recently out of a job, and putting on a brave face – a throat laugh that goes on too long, a grin that stays, as when his wife upped and left taking the kids with her and people who didn't know called 'All right, Brian!'

He tells me old Barry Moore's house (Lionel to us kids) has been boarded up, padlocked and grilled (I picture a slice of house in a toaster). Christ, didn't I hear the council making that racket this morning? Working on a Saturday, must think we're bad. Kids – not Louise or Blake, he adds quickly – are already there, spraying and smashing. I'll give 'em child abuse. Brian getting warm enough to unzip.

Then on this Saturday when everything seems to happen, music beginning to blow from every open window – Blake's – a seagull drops into Brian's pond and stabs out the goldfish one by one. Bloated, it falls in. A seagull with indigestion in a 2' by 2' pond, no response to my neighbour's shouts and handclaps. 'I wouldn't mind,' Brian says, 'but we're nowhere near the fucking sea.'

And what's this my daughter's saying to me an hour later, make-up looking weird, saying to me of her friend, 'She earns two hundred pounds a week on them chat-line things and what do I get? Seven pounds a day on stupid Community Industry.'

Seven pounds a week was my first wage and I know this can't be right thirty years later and think nothing much is right thirty years later although we all thought it would be. I feel for her – her hair making her look like something left out in the wind – but 'Those things aren't right,' I say. 'Anyway you're only sixteen.'

'She's seventeen, but she passes for older,' she says as if

this makes a difference. 'I don't look it do I?'

She wears a black and white mini which reminds me of the sixties, reminds me of Denise, but Lou's thinner. I thought at one time 'anorexic' but she – and Denise – assures me she isn't.

I go in after that to Blake's Gatling-gun rap music – at his age.

The rest of the day comes blue, bluer, bluest as the temperature rises. It's maybe the first of many such days, or more likely a one-off. All day I'm in and out of the house, getting out of it in the cooler front room looking out of the bay at the sky, blue fingers dipping down among the houses. The city centre like a fortress in a haze away to the left.

The houses round here have that grey pebbledash which cracks and falls off in slices. Stub of lawn at the front, longer at the back. Not as bad as some places – a towerblock, say – but ageing is always a problem. Not as bad as Brian makes out, I always thought, but it's looking worse than I've ever seen it in the glare of light. They used to cut the grass in the middle, place to play games in my youth, but now it's overgrown with thistles, mounds of rubbish appearing and earth and grass and flowering weeds. Young kids like tunnelling in it. Today one kid runs round and round the green, now precariously on the kerb, now off. Alexandra Stadium to him. The kids all wear baseball caps these days, American slang – Blake. (And very young girls get their hair permed – Louise.) 'Look,' I say to him when he appears slack-clothed from his music-drenched room, 'why don't you go out on a day like this? Or help in the garden?' He goes out.

When I look out later I see he's only got as far as the boarded up house. The end one at the neck, the exit/ entrance to the cul-de-sac, a bit bigger than the others, an extra bedroom and a side garden with a tree. Denise used to go by saying 'Covet, covet.' For as long as I remember it was occupied only by Barry Moore, who'd always looked the same to me: huge black eyebrows and hanks of grey hair either side of a small head (though in forty years his appearance must have changed). Lately he'd taken to stop- ping me and muttering some stuff about a football team I used to play in. It was a daily ritual, always on my way home from work, my gate in sight, and with weariness instead of blood circulating in me I'd nod him on, nod him on. I was some link to his past: we were the two remaining original occupants of 'Oxford Place, Cul-de-Sac'. Then, last week, he died.

I walk down the outdoors for some cans, but more to see what's going on around that house (there's graffiti already on one boarded up window – I LOVE MYSELF), and to have a glance at Blake. His gang are chucking stones into the middle of the green where somebody has made a little sculpture of bricks, tins and lino. At least there are no glue bags in sight. 'Pack it in,' I shout at them to no effect, although Blake stops. He nods at me like some distant acquaintance. I remember practising with a ball out on the green when they used to cut it, trying to teach him to kick with both feet. That was my trouble – I got into the school team, left midfield, but couldn't progress because I was too one-footed.

To the outdoors, looking forward to the beer, having cans in the fridge for later; Denise'll have one with me. The sunglasses of the Marlboro ad reflect a landscape not of the flyover that rises in the air above our heads, but of somewhere hotter. Desert. That outcrop of rocks Indians always hide behind.

Coming back there's a jagged hole in the empty house door. Axed through by the look, padlock still holding the frame in place. There's a boy in the tree, breaking off twigs and small branches and throwing them down. I don't recognize him. No sign of Blake.

Out the back with the beer and a lie in the sun with the newspaper. Sounds from the 'sac echoing down our entry and the occasional squawks from the fat seagull next door send me into a snooze over next week's TV. I'm woken by Denise saying the Australian results are on and I should check them. She's pulled out a deckchair and has on a bikini top and shorts. I wonder how long she's been there, and touch her neck to see how warm she is.

'Louise phoned. She's staying with 'Lex.' Alex? Isn't that the name of the friend she told me about in the garden, the one who speaks dirt down the phone? I can't help imagining what she might say. But Denise says at least she phoned, and I feel relieved it isn't worse news – I am pregnant, or I have AIDS.

Marian draws up in a K-reg car, on her way somewhere. Dressed up to show off to Denise and Louise (the two eeses, she calls them). She worries about the car, she wonders how we can live here, why don't we move now both of us are earning? Of course we've thought about it and might still, have to see how secure these jobs are. 'It's not that bad,' I say. She asks is something going on because half the street's milling about outside.

Then she settles into some office gossip, they both work at police headquarters in the city. 'Anita says, "I suppose you don't get that problem do you, at your age, the uniformed men eyeing you up?" The cheek of it.' I see the two turn and wrap themselves in slanderous conversation.

I look out for Blake. Three sets of music come from around the 'sac. Older men in unbuttoned shirts lounge on someone's step in the sun. After Marian goes we have a laugh, but Dee is thinking life can be good for a divorcee maybe and I need to touch her and see her eyes look at me square again. Of course when I sit next to her Blake drifts in.

'What's going on out there?'
'Nutten.'

Brian comes round too, should we call the police? Apparently they were round earlier. Brian says we should at least get Blake away, and although I think it will come to nothing, we decide it might be for the best. I ring my brother across the city and he says fine, Blake can stay. He will enjoy it, we think, thrashing his cousin at Sonic Hedgehog ('Sonic the Hedgehog,' he corrects me). But he's reluctant and we bribe him – Dee's idea – with a stop at the drive-in McDonald's, not long open and still of interest to him.

We drive round on the ring road to the big yellow M. I give our orders to the hatted girl behind the automatic window and moan to wife and son: 'America!'

'This used to be a cinema.' I say this every time we pass here, and say it now to tease Blake. Denise and I swap titles of films we saw when we were 'courting'. *'Barbarella.' 'Midnight Cowboy.' '2001.'*

'Your mother was a film fanatic, we were the only couple that didn't snog.'

When we get the order we drive to the car park, eat our Big Macs and watch other cars come and go. It's still blue outside. I share a milkshake with Dee. We can't resist cigarettes. We, who love smoke curling from our mouths too much and forget about the smell and the stain and the lung damage. We'll reform, we'll stop, we'll do it, we say – and the years pass.

'Open the window then.' Blake disgusted.

We drop him off all right and drive back feeling light. 'Shall I stop for some more cans?' I say. Which we do.

Then, when we're nearing a lane I know that loops down behind a garage and ends at the canal, I say 'Do you want to park up?' Denise laughs – it was what was said after those cinema nights when, still discussing the film, she'd give me what I missed in those back rows and more. We sit silent for a while at this unexpectedness, and then relive a long ago night with its early slow caress and fiddling with clothes. She ends up on top, not moving much, jammed on to me, head bent with the roof. We swap teenage giggles, hold each other steady. When I've come I notice her eyes look down on me and wonder if she's seeing all the days since that first time in the car – and what she makes of it all. Us.

We come apart slowly, in stages. We're happy as we rejoin the road. But blue light and sirens, a fire engine and police riot vans force us to park up again. And when we get moving a helicopter comes steadily above – with a searchlight making shop fronts brilliant. It swings over the rooftops. We turn off and there is the rocking machine, balanced at an angle on its cone of light, above our corner.

The police are erecting a barrier and say we can't get in the 'sac now. Overturned cars are across the entrance, I recognize Brian's. I look out at bands of policemen, shields resting on the vans, milling amongst the vehicles.

'What will you do?' Denise asks across me; she knows the policeman from work.

'Take it easy, see what happens.'

He won't tell us much about what's happening in there, just keeps advising us to go elsewhere. We drive off but decide to circle round and come into the estate another way. Denise reckons Pat will let us through her back garden – if the police aren't there – and we can get into Brian's and then our own.

Pat thinks we're mad to go back – 'Stay here the night!' We hurry through the gardens and although it's not yet quite dark I misjudge a jump and get a sogger in Brian's empty pool. No sign of him.

When we get into our place I see the Cherie Lunghi film finishing – we've left the television on. My insides are sliding as we go to the front window and stand side by side to watch what is outside.

A whole industry going on out there, people buzzing around Barry Moore's house. Not only kids as you might think, but the adults who've finally had enough of waiting for the break, of keeping themselves and their kids occupied, and now organize them in the dismantling of the house.

People carry out doors, chopped up stairs in bundles, window frames and skirting boards. They throw them on the fire on the green, half the size of a house and boosted by unwanted furniture, fences, the tree in lengths, and set fire to with syphoned petrol probably from the overturned cars. Flame bearing heat to every surrounding window shoots up. This on a day still hot and light pouring down from a helicopter. A cheer goes up as the helicopter moves up and across out of the way of a high-reaching flame. That's done it, I think, the police will pile in now. I'm wondering what to do and notice something familiar on the TV screen. 'Look,' I say to Denise. I'm seeing what I never thought I would see. Live TV pictures from our corner.

Come See About Me

I was all right until Wednesday, I'd kept things at bay. Then Andy called and began everything again. As usual I was doing my job of ten years staring at the brick wall opposite, waiting for customers. I had the sports pages open to the side of me but I'd already read them twice. I had a cold or something, a headache. Down the corridor the door opened, letting in the oily smell of the loading bay, and I heard a voice ask, 'Through here?'

Just before they reach me I always wonder what customers will make of me, framed as I am, head and shoulders in a wall, and I always pick up a pen, look busy.

'Well Goal-ie,' this man said, 'it's you.'

I knew before I looked up it was Andy. A feeling like a hunger pang twisted down through me. I sneezed, swabbed my nose and said, speaking to him for the first time in over twenty years, 'Can't be.' I pretended to look more closely at him. 'It is, though. Andy.'

Andy's not his real name, he's one of the Andersons from the south-west of the city, where I'm from. Nobody liked them much on the estate – there were too many of them, cousins everywhere, and always involved in gang fights and petty crime. Andy's elder brother, for instance, was forever in and out of Winson Green on assault charges. (I know because my mother drove their mother, a huge woman who sighed a lot, to the prison while I sat in the back peering out at the man in uniform who didn't come halfway up the huge, bolt-studded doors.) But Andy was weak and pale, double-jointed, harmless.

'How's your brother, Andy?' I gave him a smile.

'Out, out you know. 'S doing well.' He gave me one back – the same old gappy grin, now beneath a scratchy blond moustache.

He was still thin, his shoulders still sloped, his donkey jacket hung off him. At school he was an outcast but I was his friend because of his younger sister. She was as thin as him, but dark and twice as good looking. I thought she was lovely. She must have been eleven or twelve the time I knew her. Brown hair and brown legs. Her hair was short, mostly tied back with a bit of ribbon. I'm talking of a long time ago now, but you don't forget your first love. Linda.

I couldn't bring myself to ask after her though I don't think Andy knew anything ever happened between us and nothing much did really.

Only this:

Andy's dad was a drunk and he had a job delivering

cakes to shops. The brown van with the red LYONS stamp was often parked outside their house. (The Andersons lived on cakes, Andy always smelt of milk, chocolate and dirt like some infant.) Sometimes on his dad's return from a Saturday lunchtime session when he would often lie on the sofa in a stupor, Andy was able to steal his keys and take us – me and Linda – into the van. We would take only one box each, so he wouldn't notice, of our favourite cakes.

Then one Saturday Linda opened the door, saying that Andy had to go down the shops; she also said I should be very quiet and let me in. 'Wait here,' she said and opened the door to the living room. Inside I could see Mr Anderson, a short but broad man with very black hair, sat on a chair, his boots only just touching the floor. At first I thought he was looking directly at me but then I realized his eyes were closed. He had his elbow propped on one of those old radio sets, nearly as tall as Linda. There was no carpet on the floor so Linda, light anyway, tiptoed towards him. I could see the keys on top of the set which was reporting on a Villa match. I was afraid for her: I saw flecks of white at the man's mouth, and the strong hair-matted fist propping his cheek. At the same time her movement – tiptoe, tiptoe, her breath held, her face shining with purpose – made me go fierce inside. Fourteen-year-old fierce. She lifted the keys slowly; her father muttered and moved as she did but she didn't flinch.

We flew down the path laughing, I remember it as a whirl of pink skirt and brown skin. We got inside the van and shut the door, and in the dark groped around for the cakes we liked. We were both after the almond slices. She found them first and offered me the box. All I could see were her eyes, her socks and her smile, and I kissed the dark arm that held the box. We sat on the floor squeezed between the metal racks and ate. She allowed me two lip-kisses. We hugged each other, I felt all her small body, her long legs with my hands. We just ate one box. When we got out we hid behind the hedge because we could see Andy at the window looking out, and we made our way down the entry to the back of the house. It was, is, the last street in Birmingham and directly behind it is a foothill of the Lickeys. We climbed a little way up and hid ourselves in a hollow burnt out tree there and watched the sky move overhead. Or that's how I remember it now.

And that was all.

'You still lib there then,' I said to him, referring to the address on the parcel. The same house I saw Linda steal the keys.

We talked a bit, and even though I'd moved out of the area years before, he somehow knew I was divorced with one son. I found out he had three boys – Rick, Mark and Shaun – and a ten-year-old marriage.

'Good to see you, Andy,' I found myself saying as he signed the form, head down. His hair was thin but showed no sign of balding. 'We'll hab to get togebber and talk ober old times.'

'Yes,' he said, turning, parcel under his arm. There was a council stamp on his jacket. 'Bad cold you got there.' I listened to him walk down the corridor. As he opened the door, he called, 'Rich-iee.' And then, again, that nickname.

Goalie. I was dubbed that after my father who played 'keeper for Walsall FC for a while when he was younger.

(Some of the newcomers, hearing the nickname, confuse me with him although he retired from the post office eight years ago, and ask me what it was like out on the pitch, and was I ever on telly.) My dad was popular. He used to stride around the estate in his track suit bouncing a ball, me running beside him in my kit, gathering kids from their front lawns, taking them down the park and setting up a game. He had a whistle. Even at that time he played for the PO team, top of the league thanks to his famous 'clean sheets'. There is the picture of him, they still have it somewhere. He is in a dive, three feet above the ground, long shorts. He's laid out in the air like a sleeper, muddy knees bent, eyes shut, his head lying on his outstretched arm that has the ball at the end like someone has put it in his hand. I spent my early years trying to do just that, lie in the air and save the day, be a hero as easily as that.

People knew us on that estate, and not only because of Dad. Mum was a semi-professional hairdresser, she used to drive round to her customers, equipment stacked in the boot. (With two incomes we were one of the first families on the estate to have a car.) She kept wigs on white polystyrene heads in the kitchen on which I'd draw thin blue moustaches, the biro sticking, pulling out membranes from the perfect upper lip.

Some women came to the house for their cuts and perms, including 'Mother' Anderson – that's how I first met Andy. There were magazines around and comics for the kids. Dad used to complain it was like a 'Women's Bloody Institute' but I liked all the laughter and chat and Mum singing as she went about her work. (I've always liked to hear singing, especially women singing; I used to be a big pop fan.) When beehives came in there were cans of lacquer everywhere and our food used to taste of it.

I remember once bringing Andy round and she offered him a sausage roll – recipe from the Be-Ro cookbook – and asked how was his 'poor old mum'. He looked up with those vague blue eyes, finding it strange but comforting (I think now) that someone should ask such things.

You see what I mean about Andy's visit starting everything again? And it didn't stop there, unfortunately. My cold or whatever it was got worse and worse until I couldn't bear the sight of the bricks any longer and I locked the hatch and hobbled down to the office.

The boss had eyes enough to see I was in no fit state. I was shivering, although I was hot, shivering and snivelling before him. He didn't give me any what-is-the-world-coming-to, he advised me to go straight to the doctor.

I went straight home.

I got in, I felt dead. I'm not kidding. I was all blocked up one side – nostril, ear, brain. I put my finger up to my ear and discovered this black wax coming out, almost runny. And my digestive system started to kick and buckle. I couldn't face my boil-in-the-bag curry. Instead I sat in the kitchen for what seemed hours listening to the fridge turn on and off. I watched the woman next door collect washing in the early dusk and found my memories had moved on to Jackie, my ex-wife.

There were three phases with Jackie – courtship/early marriage, man on the moon and divorce. The first was the best and started when we were still at school. We met at youth club dances where they played Tamla Motown and we both discovered a taste for it. I started buying the records (still did up until a few years ago) and me and Jackie would play them up in my room. We'd watch *Ready Steady Go* cheering any Tamla. She liked Marvin Gaye and Stevie Wonder but I went for those girl groups, Martha and the Vandellas, the Supremes. The early stuff. Dancing with their elbows high. Dad thought I was mad ('screeching coloured girls in wigs' he called them). Mum knew what it was about, she advised me on clothes.

Despite this madness Dad put in a good word for me at work (although not high up in the post office, he was respected) – and I became a postman. Not long after that we married and my room became our home. Still too young to go to pubs we went to dances and cinemas. We saw *Goldfinger* maybe a dozen times, just to get out of the place and be together. Gliding home on the bus along the tree-lined Bristol Road I would be Sean Connery and she Honor Blackman.

I'm saying that these memories ran in sequence, like reels of a film, which is not strictly true, but they did more or less. At some point I dragged myself into the front room and switched on the TV – *Wogan*, *Dallas* and whatnot a blur to me – as they continued.

Later man walked on the moon and I was optimistic. Jackie was pregnant with Ben and we were given a council house. (Birmingham too was booming – it was the time of the Mini, plenty of work at nearby Longbridge where they made that car. A few years before the Rotunda and all the other towerblocks had been erected along with Spaghetti Junction and the Bull Ring shopping centre – who was to know then how much they'd be hated now?)

Work interferes with your social life, and working early is worse. I started to resent having to get up each morning for the round, especially in those cold, pre-central heating days, leaving her warmly wrapped in bed. Jealousy I suppose. One of the strongest pictures I have of Jackie is one shoulder showing like an island among the dark hair flowing over the pillow. A glimpse of her profile as I dressed by the light of a streetlamp. We were still going out a lot, out of habit, and sometimes we'd get back so late it was hardly worthwhile me going to bed. We'd fallen in with this older couple who took us out to pubs, clubs and discotheques (a new word then) that played soul. We popped a few pills with them, drank too much, danced. Afterward we might all end up in one of the Indian restaurants that were opening up. I had this vague notion that we would do this in turn, guide a younger couple, show them 'around'. Huh. They, the older pair, moved away. Seven or eight years later he returned, bearded and divorced.

I knew something was up, but not that. I didn't know exactly what was going on until that night she told me I was a dust-collecting object.

At the time I'd moved to the sorting office and I'd let the job's routine – which at first I liked, better than freezing on the round, I thought – get on top of me. Maybe I was getting dull, stuck in my ways. I still liked Tamla but she had no time for it – 'teenage stuff' she called it and I couldn't play it when she was in the house. When she was out (visiting him I now know) and I'd got Ben off to sleep, I'd compile tapes of my favourites, often changing the order. Diana Ross's 'Come See About Me' was the last song I recorded while my wife was making escape plans, was moving out. She had the whole thing planned, down to removal men being hired. I sat alone in the house while strangers asked me where to find items on a list and struggled at getting beds through doorways.

I've had nearly ten years of this life ever since. In charge of the undelivered at work and at home my own company. I almost prefer the last stage to this, the time of excuses and sulks and arguments; at least Ben was here, and I could talk to him. I can't now, not properly, I'm a figure from his past.

That night I couldn't sleep. The bed seemed to tilt. The way my stomach heaved I felt sure I was going to hatch an alien like in the video. I heard voices, laughter, noises. I thought, this is it, I've cracked. I thought I'd hear these voices for ever. One was Jackie's getting louder and louder repeating the same phrase, 'You and who else?' Another was Andy's boyhood voice threatening to kill me. On top of this were odd bits of music and adverts – 'Jimmy Mac' mixed with 'Get the Maximum out of Life'.

It was afternoon before I finally got up. Bloody black wax was still coming out of my ear and it was hard to breathe. I went down to evening surgery. The doctor, a thin, elderly woman who peered at me over the top of her glasses as if baffled by my existence, listened to my chest, looked down my weeping ear. Straightening up, complaining of lumbago, she said I had an infection and prescribed antibiotics.

They must have done some good for the following day, today, I felt fit enough to go out and get a video. That's where I met Andy again, busy sweeping leaves outside the shops. At first I didn't see it was him and later realized I must have seen him before picking up things with that metal instrument, sweeping.

He called me over. 'Seen that,' he said. I had *Lethal Weapon* in my hand. 'It's good.'

He leaned against his yellow truck. Some dusty blond hair came through a hole in his woollen hat. 'You're in a bad way,' he said to me. 'Been to the quack's? Whad'ee say?'

'An infection, says I've got an infection.'

'Is it catching?' He moved back, grinning. His face had picked up the same creases as his dad's.

'I don't know.'

Wind flapped our trousers. I tapped the video against my leg.

'You've not changed much,' he said eventually. (It's not true.) 'We should get together and have that chat. You know where, don't you? Still in the old place.'

'What, Linda too?' I couldn't help asking.

'No, I mean the wife and me, Helen. And the chavvies.' He told me again about his three boys, and gave me his phone number which he wrote on a torn off piece of fag packet he picked off the ground.

When I got back my back window was wide open but I didn't think what it could mean until I got into the front room, video in hand and no VCR to put it in.

Not only did they take the video, they took the TV, the hi-fi, and my Tamla collection. The contents of my jacket pockets were spread across the table: keys, travelcard, a picture of Ben with his CSE certificates, notes from work, old payslips. I didn't ring the police, there was no point, I wasn't insured. All I did was put a nail through the window catch and sit down.

I sat with my arms folded, letting go to my illness. I started sweating and aching all over. The room seemed to get thin somehow, with all the empty spaces where the machines had been. Voices came again, Ben saying clearly he was going to get married.

I had to get out of the house. I could have gone down the pub, there's a few of us single blokes meet up now and then (the talk starts on sport and sex but usually gets round to shopping), but I didn't fancy that. I could have gone round my folks but I didn't want to worry them.

It was only later I thought of Andy, remembered his number in my pocket.

'I had a burglary,' I told him on the phone, 'just after I saw you. They took my video.'

'Oh no,' he said. 'Then you can't see it.'

'What?'

'Lethal Weapon.'

'No.' A pause. Then I sighed. 'I don't know, Andy. Something bad always happens this time of year.' I started rabbiting, ending up with 'Things seem to go wrong for me lately.'

'Do they?' he said. I could tell he wasn't used to the phone, had been amazed to be called to it by his wife. But he gathered, somehow, what I wanted. 'Come up and watch it on our video if you want. Bring it with you.'

'What?'

'Lethal Weapon.'

*

I stood on their corner for a while, looked down this last street of the city. Clouds like smoke rose off the hills behind the houses. I'd forgotten how quiet it was but I hadn't forgotten the look of it. It has changed all around, with silvery towerblocks one side and cul-de-sacs of new houses on the other, but that street was the same. I expected to see the cake van parked on the corner and Dad with his special green gloves bouncing a ball. I recalled waiting in the car while Mum in her hairdo and two-piece suit helped Mrs Anderson down the step, and Linda running down the path with me, dangling the keys.

I walked towards their number remembering the last time I'd called there. It was after Andy's father had found out about the cakes and given him a real beating. (Mum told me about it.) It was his brother, out of prison at the time, who opened the door. 'He ain't coming out, Goalie.' 'Oh,' I said. 'I wouldn't bother coming back,' he added kindly.

Andy's wife was the image of Linda. A shock. At first I thought it was her, but I could see she was too young – mid to late twenties – for that. But she had her face, her hair, her shape, or what I thought would be her face, hair, shape if I saw her again. While I was being introduced everything about her stirred up a memory of Andy's sister. In the course of the conversation I realized they were cousins. Andy had stayed a bachelor until he was thirty but the family had got him married off to Helen when she was sixteen (same age as Jackie when we married). It was like an arranged marriage. It was an arranged marriage.

The next thing to strike me was being in a house with kids. Everywhere there was evidence of them – toys, washing drying on a radiator, comics. The three boys were got out of bed to greet the visitor. They didn't see many strangers. I could see they were curious, although the eldest hung back. The middle one had a broken arm, an edge of dirty plaster came out of the sleeve of his dressing gown. The youngest, chubby and blond, soon climbed on my lap and swung his legs. He asked me questions.

'Are you bald?' He touched my receding hairline.

Helen laughed but said, 'Shaun, stop fretting Daddy's friend.' It seemed ages since I'd heard a woman laugh.

''S all right,' I said. To the boy I said, 'Yeh, I'm a bald old coot.'

'Is coot a bad word?'

The middle one, who stood by my chair lank and serious looking, said, 'Shut up, stupid.'

'Are you an uncle?'

'Of course he isn't, stupid.'

Eventually Helen took the kids off to bed. I leaned forward, made a motion like turning a key in a lock.

'How's your brother, Andy?' I kept my face serious.

He laughed, this time aloud. 'Out, out.'

We talked about our families. His dad was dead from booze, his mother lived with one of her sisters. He didn't mention Linda. Then he asked about the burglary. All the time I was aware of his wife upstairs, trying to get the kids into bed. In this house Linda had lived, this was the room she'd tiptoed across, she had played here, dried her hair by the fire, had grown up to look like Helen, surely.

'That video,' Andy said, 'd'you bring it?'

'Yes.' I wasn't interested any more but had brought the video because it made an excuse for coming. 'But don't bother, you've seen it . . .'

''Sno bother.' On his bony knees he bent to the player, like a Moslem at prayer, and ejected one. 'You got it?'

I handed it over.

'What else did they take?'

'Sorry?'

'The burglars.'

'Oh, TV, hi-fi, you know, and my Tamla.'

'Your what?'

'Motown . . . records, they took my records.'

'Hear that, Hel?' She was coming in the room with a tray. 'They stole his certificates too.'

'He means music records.' I watched her come in, put down the tray. 'Have some crisps.' She pushed a breakfast bowl of cheese and onion (I can tell by the colour) across the table. 'I like Tamla, I'm a soul fan.'

'Are you?'

'Yes, I've got some, but I like modern stuff better – Lionel Richie, Michael Jackson. Do you like him?'

'Yes,' I lied. 'He was with Tamla, as part of the Jackson Five.'

'Hear that?' she said to her husband. 'Rich likes Michael Jackson.' To me, 'He hates it.'

The way she said 'Rich' made me realize Andy, who used to call me that, had been talking about me. I also realized that she wouldn't know him as Andy and I searched my memory for his real name – Philip or Peter?

Then she started telling me of groups she had seen at New Street Odeon, dragging a reluctant Andy along, but with the kids she hadn't been for a while. I tried to imagine Andy there, an odd person among the fashionably dressed – he must have hated it. I thought of this as I watched her talk, listening to the up and down of her voice, watching her dark brown eyes darken as she became excited.

To keep her talking I told her all I knew about the early Michael Jackson, how Diana Ross had watched the family audition and had promised to take an interest in their careers, and how this had led to him wanting to look like, to be Diana Ross. It was funny talking music; I thought of music as something that dropped out of you, the rhythms becoming meaningless, but of course she was much younger. I was over forty and talking pop. It was because I saw what I had only seen once in a woman before, I saw that she was interested in me, I saw she liked me.

Andy started the video and went out to get some home brew. She sat down, I could feel her eyes keep looking over at me as the trailers came up. Although the illness was still plugged deep in me, making everything seem a little blocked, fused together, although I still felt pain in my side and head, I felt another, a new sensation, and the best way to describe it is my nerves, all, felt comfortable.

Andy brought in three pints in his stretched hands. The beer looked weak, no head.

'This is the stuff,' he said. He was anxious to know what I thought of it. I took a few swallows, it wasn't weak.

The film had started and Andy began telling me the plot – see him, he's a bit mad, he jumps off this building – but I didn't mind. I hardly took in the film which was another of those American movies where there's a good cop and a bad one. The bad one was bad because he'd lost his wife and didn't care what he did.

We watched, sipped, had another and another. I got a bit drunk. I think the alcohol reacted with the pills. Inside the house, I was thinking, appearing on the doorstep like a waif. I remembered how this room had looked that day she stole the keys. No carpet then, a rug by the metal-blue stove, and the big old radio. Things have changed so much since, it seemed it couldn't possibly have ever been like that.

When I went up to the toilet I was fascinated by the women's things there. Not many, but enough. I slid the double mirror door open and looked at Tampax, cotton buds, most of all shampoo and conditioner. (My mother still does hair – some pensioners in a nearby sheltered accommodation, and they walk round with late fifties cuts.) I glanced at a Mills and Boon on the windowsill. 'He folded his long legs into the sleek new sports car and turned the ignition', the story began. On the way down I looked in through a bedroom door. Two beds, two small heads I made out.

At the end of the film Andy went out again with the glasses.

'Let's stick some music on,' she said. 'What do you fancy?'

It was her turn to get down on the floor. I looked and looked as she searched through the collection. She turned her head and said to come down and so I did, knelt beside her and for the first time I felt her warmth. I touched her arm.

'Do you know Linda?'

'Not very well,' she said, her face close. 'You know she emigrated before I married Paul.'

'Did she?' I could imagine her doing that. 'To Australia?'

'Canada. Didn't you know? I thought Paul said . . .'

We heard Andy – Paul his name was of course – coming back, and she quickly pulled a record out. This movement told me more than anything.

'Five Star?' She was showing me the cover as he came in, slowly, with another three pints.

'You really like this stuff?' Andy winced as the music started.

Helen stood up. 'He does. He's said he does. Next time he comes we'll have a music night.'

Next time, next time.

Andy was grinning at me, but then he squinted. 'You all right?'

I nodded but I did feel a bit sickly then and a minute later I left the room. I had intended to go upstairs but instead I turned and went into the kitchen. It had a smell of fry-ups. A chip pan sat on a back burner, its wire basket half embedded in lard. I hadn't seen that since I was a kid.

I was drunk but it wasn't like being drunk at all. Through the kitchen window was the dark shape of the hill, one or two lights near the top. The city seemed miles away. On that hill I'd tasted almond crumbs in her mouth.

I could hear them talking about me in the other room, their voices hardly dropped, against the background of bright pop music.

'Is he all right d'you think?' I heard Helen say.

I was stood right over the oven. I put my fingers into the grey flecked lard, lifted them to my nose. The smell set off my whole nervous system, a spasm. I held on hard to it but I had to close my eyes. When I opened them again I saw Andy in the doorway watching me, puzzled.

Betty and Brian

When I was forty my mother married again. It wasn't exactly wedding of the year. The bridegroom arrived on a bicycle and stuttered his 'I do'. The registrar, who only visited the town on Fridays, looked benign and official, but when he smiled he had a tooth missing. The guests were few and rum, and the bridesmaid, Aunty Maureen, farted.

Outside everybody lit up fags, including me, and cupped them out of sight for the photographs. There was a slight drizzle. We got mixed up with the previous couple's party on the steps of the red-brick building which also housed, according to plaques, the library and the dentist's. When they'd gone, a much brighter bunch than us, it was sad to see how small a crowd we were. Father's been dead years, and recently Mum's sisters, all but Maureen, had died, and my sister couldn't come, couldn't get back from the US where she lives with husband and kids. There weren't many on his side either. There was one morose child of about seven who appeared round people's legs, a white face shaped like India. Normally I avoid children, but they brighten up occasions like these. Mum talked to me hesitantly as if afraid her voice might break something.

At the reception, in the skittle alley of a small hotel round the corner, I talked to him, Brian. He was defensive, polite, that occasional stutter. West country with an overlay of cockney. His suit had large brown and grey checks. One hand held his pint, the other fingered his carnation or rubbed his nose. He looked myopic, as if the world consisted of ten feet around him, and was surprised to find me in that space. I tried to put him at his ease. I'd only met him once before, briefly, he was leaving as I arrived at Mum's one night. (I'd said to her later 'Was that your boyfriend?' and she'd said no.) I put my hand on his arm.

'Well, well,' I said, couldn't think of anything else, 'you're saddled with Mum.' A joke, but it didn't come out right. I started again, 'You're my . . .' and couldn't say it. I looked down. By his large polished shoes, tied with double bows, a nub end and a cocktail stick.

We were all up one end of the alley near a small hatch, metal shutter raised, one beer pump and a basket with packets of crisps. You could see into the bar beyond, dark and empty – it was about 4.30. People's shoes squeaked on the floor as they moved. There were three small groups standing and some at tables. The talk was low. I didn't know where Mum was. I heard someone say 'that mort' and the beginnings of a laugh but it died. Down the side of the alley were three or four tables covered with red crêpe and plates and bowls of drumsticks, sandwiches, crisps and pork pie with egg in it.

We got talking at last. We swapped work stories. He'd just retired in fact from the railways. 'I've been about,' he said, 'north-east run mainly, London, Newcastle, Edinburgh. I've lived in London too.' He pronounced it Lon-durn.

We talked of north of the river and south of the river and the difference there is. He didn't know my part. 'But I always wanted to get back here,' he said. 'I was born here.' A small, river-soaked town. Had I seen the floods? I had, a sheet of it glinting across half a field as I came by in a taxi. Crossing the bridge I looked along the back of shops and pubs, gardens and walls that sloped down to the river bank. He said March and April were the worst, when the floods were known to reach the houses. He talked rugby next, had to drive miles to see a decent match. I knew nothing of that but nodded.

'Are you a lager lout?' I asked him when there was a pause. He looked shocked. 'What I mean is, can I get you one in?' I wasn't doing very well.

Made my way through a room of thin red lips (the women had slapped it on like some of the boys at the club), and the few men, who were struck with age as if by something sharp. Leaning on the counter I heard crying from somewhere in the building, and it wasn't a child's. The barman made no comment as he poured, eyes on his work. I wished my sister had been able to come with her husband and kids.

I'd hoped someone would have joined the groom but I

found him in the same spot, alone. We sipped. He called Mum Betty, which was odd: to most people she was Liz. I asked him was he married before and I thought I'd heard he was but he said no, a bachelor all his life. But not, he assured me, one of them. I thought of Peter back home and what he might be doing when I said, 'Yes, I'm a bachelor too.'

Finally Mother arrived. She'd been looking for Aunty Maureen, she explained, who seemed to have disappeared on the way to the hotel. Brian said it was impossible to get lost in this town and she'd turn up soon. Mum said he didn't know Aunty Maureen.

Brian stood as upright as he could which was not very. His face showed that he was, or had been, a drinker. It was what I expected. I said how did they meet, and she said Brian was a wrestling fan too, they'd met at a contest. I thought, in the bar. I remembered wet Saturdays, having to stay in, wrestling on *World of Sport* as washing dried in front of the fire. On the principle of can't beat them, Mum drank and booed Mick McManus while Dad drank and cheered a stripper in another part of town. Me and my sister, too old for it really, argued who was someone's best best friend, me or her.

'I'm glad I don't have to make a speech,' I said: she'd said not on the phone. Just a quiet do she'd said. Something in the evening though, as she hadn't seen me for a while and that would 'make a day of it'. They wouldn't be off (she didn't say honeymoon) until tennish. She'd booked me and Aunty Maureen rooms in the hotel.

'Maybe some dancing though,' Brian unexpectedly said. 'Maybe some dancing later on.'

*

And later a few more people did turn up, and a real disco with a Brummie DJ – the shaved-above-the-ears type – and two sets of lights. They'd covered the alley with boards. Some of the locals came round from the bar. It was a long time since I'd seen so many men with sideburns and patterned shirts. The green stripe of Woodbine on the tables. But some younger ones turned up later, attracted by the music.

In the old tradition bride and groom danced first. Kind of waltzed to Barry White. They moved through the green red blue, both small people, five two apiece. Then they sat down and for two or three numbers the floor remained empty and we all sat looking at it.

Brian went for drinks. Mum said, 'What do you think?'

'Of Brian?'

'Yes.' She leaned forward and all her years showed, came to the edge of her flesh. 'Honestly now.'

Behind her two refugees from a youth club had got up to dance to Kylie Minogue. The girl danced on chip-fed legs. I studied the boy. 'He seems right fine to me.' A term we used ironically of my father. 'No, he's all right.'

Mum used to be a looker, jet black hair and eyes to match. My father was always sloping off for days, mostly with other women or up to some scam, and there was no shortage of men willing to step into the space he left. But she would have none of them, not even at her drunkest. Like everyone else she adored my father. After he'd died – of a heart attack at thirty-nine – people would come up and tell me what a wonderful man he was. I was a teenager then and would snort in their faces. They admired his audacity – he was always up to some scheme or other – and his 'capacity for life'. They meant his capacity for drink. They saw him drunk and generous; we saw him drunk and mean. Or recovering and mean. He used to come home when his money ran out, like an invalid, limping. Mum would attend to him, take soup and stuff up to him and try and keep us two quiet. He'd come out of it, come round, with new plans in his mind. He'd be on the telephone, send me out with messages. His mates would call round, blokes with wet coats that would pile up in our room, mine and Susie's, and we'd rifle the pockets. Mum would make tea for them or, more likely, open bottles. Then, having got loans or collected debts, he'd leave us some – never enough – money, and be gone again.

'He helps with the housework,' she said.

'Does he? That's a good sign.' It is. At the start our housework was shared, though neglect was more our forte. Sometimes, enthusiastic, we'd take the polish and duster, one each, work together. (But guess who got the duster?)

I put my arm round her. She felt fragile, meek under the dress. The white dots in that odd light seemed to lift off the dress and float between us. I thought of insects, something buzzing. Her black hair has turned really white, as mine is beginning to do, but she'd put some kind of rinse on it, I couldn't tell what colour in this room.

'Everything'll be good,' I said, as if I knew. 'You enjoy yourself here after the dirty old Smoke.'

Brian came back with more drinks and I made more of an effort to include him. We had a half-heard conversation about their new home, a bungalow. He was concerned I had the right address and spent a good ten minutes giving me directions, pointing out short cuts and hazardous junctions. I didn't like to tell him I didn't drive.

The DJ had begun putting on more disco tracks. No hi-energy stuff which I imagined Pete to be leaping about to at that very minute, but things like Yazz and Neneh Cherry, and more and more of this town's youth were cutting it on the floor. Brian was tapping his feet.

'Music all right for you then?'

'Got a beat,' he conceded, rubbing his nose.

'Why don't you two dance?' I said and they didn't need much encouragement. They danced now in a semblance of a sixties style, half twist, half something of their own devising. I watched them disappear among the more limber youth.

I slipped out for a smoke. Pete was the one who got me smoking again after years without. He's one of those blokes who always carry a bit round with them. He keeps it in his shirt pocket. Starts rolling as you talk to him. Gives you a look at the joint – see, it's only a small one – shrugs, laughs and lights up.

On the way I passed through the hall, sticky faded carpet, vague smell of Chinese takeaways and stale beer. There were crates under the stairs. I thought of my room up there and the cold night ahead. Wondered if I couldn't slip away now, but it was twelve miles to the station. I passed Aunty Maureen, singing to herself. I said hello but I don't think she recognized me.

There was a door ajar, just past the stairs. I stopped to look through, wondering if this was where the crying came from earlier. The back of someone's head, a woman, watching TV. I could see the screen – Richard Widmark and Ida Lupino. 'Suzie, are you hurt?' in the mist. A blonde lies in the bushes. 'Hurry, Pete, hurry.' Widmark, obscure, starts that laugh of his. Pete would know what the film was called.

I moved on past the toilets, where cisterns, taps, a whole plumbing system was gurgling and whistling like delirious soccer fans at a referee's mistake. It died slowly. I thought of Chelsea boys with scarves tied at their wrists. I went out into the air. More of the hotel's debris, boxes, barrels and bins, lined the wall. There was a kind of courtyard at the back which gave way to trees. The hotel – really a glorified pub on the edge of town – was on three sides; one long whitewashed arm held the skittle alley, the other, shorter, housed the toilets. A black metal staircase zigzagged down the back of the main building. A light high on this wall feebly highlighted the drizzle and I went through it, across the courtyard and into the trees. My feet slithered and crunched on dropped conkers and their casings. The trunk was damp and the leaves messy so I squatted and, balancing lighter, cigarettes and papers on my knee, began rolling.

I often do this, end up out the back at parties, not often among trees, more usually dustbins and walls. Last time it was a lawn in Kilburn, lying on the wet grass, vomit spewn out in front of my eyes. Above that glistening pink pile the party on its side. That day Pete had argued and argued for no apparent reason except – he said – I wouldn't let him alone to paint. (He fancies himself as an artist.) Not true, he could have done that rather than argue, I told him. Go and paint now, I said, and he said I was stupid you couldn't just go and paint like turning on a tap. Then at the party, early on, he was kissing this other guy. Just being friendly, he said.

This time, not sick or even dizzy, enclosed in a damp den, I rolled – just a little one, but put a lot of dope in it. I could hear the swollen river lapping, absorbing drizzle with a hiss. Like something lightly frying. I smoked.

I hate to see him like that, mouth thinned out and the brows right down over his eyes. Doesn't become him, told him as much.

Somewhere over by the bins under the fire escape I heard movement, heard 'D'you want to or not? You fucking said.' A gruff voice, made so by years of smoking and drinking, I can tell that. The woman's voice was indistinct, but I heard 'You're pissed.' A bin lid clattered to the ground. One of my new in-laws, I thought, with someone else's wife.

I looked down at my suit trousers, a little wet at the hems, otherwise all right. When I looked up again I saw Mum pass a window in the corridor leading to the toilets. A narrow, long window so I saw her profile travel a slot. A little blurred by the rain. I couldn't tell by her expression how she was. I said to myself, how are you, Momma? I smoked and waited for her to return. The joint was wet and I had to keep lighting it.

The two emerged from under the stairs, appeared briefly in the courtyard and slipped into the hotel. I thought, finished already? Then the plumbing started again, whistling and jeering. I thought again of sister Sue, the boyfriend I scared off from her, and her husband John, and smiled, shifted on my floor of conkers. Then Mum reappeared, moving steadily, eyes up this time and a little smile on her face, maybe. I finished the joint and went in to see them off.

King

In the summer, when he comes home, they put him out the back. He is all right in a deckchair, he seems happiest in that.

At first Mary, his mother, was worried – what if anything happened? – always flying to him at the slightest twitch, asking him unanswerable questions – 'Are you all right, Mike?' – but with each summer as his face filled and changed she grew used to his presence and his few actions. She marked down his height using, as he was never straight, the yard-long tape coiled in the cutlery drawer. He had almost outgrown it.

Now she thought she could tell, as with the newborn or the senile, when he was hungry, cold, irritated, content and so on from the tiny grimaces he made. She felt he recognized her now when they brought him for two weeks in every year to the terraced house with their bottles of drugs and instructions. She felt some, ever so slight, progress was being made.

Moulded, burnt on to his leg, is a round scar. Born with it. His father, John, thought 'Branded, scabbed', but didn't say so. Mary thought 'Like an electricity failure' and did say. One time he thought she would talk of nothing else, curled on the sofa reading medical books all day and discussing it in bed.

Before, he'd seen James Cagney on TV and felt like him in *White Heat* – at the centre of things, even in prison. He wore a long coat and had a key job in a factory. He held court among the ever-pumping machines, gesturing with his stained hands, and the eyes of the men would follow, their ears straining to hear him above the noise.

They'd married young but were careful, planned, the baby prepared for, discussed, for several years. He came home to cooking and TV, his wife's smile: famous in the district. Money wasn't tight, there were holidays abroad, every other year a new car, nights out. But things don't last.

The factory closed. Mike. Mary started writing letters to girlfriends she knew from school. He found one: '. . . I slump in front of the television . . . the effort is too much . . . I wish I could see you, what you're up to . . . I feel squeezed up.' He knew it was him, blocking the house at that time, reading the paper, drinking coffee and smoking all day.

He got other jobs, temporary. Waiter, packer, building site dogsbody. He'd been a hospital porter. Had to wheel a body to the morgue, from surgery, an unsuccessful operation. As they rolled it into the drawer the stitches gave and blood spread along all one side of the bandages.

Now he's found a permanent job, in an office, work he's not used to; he's hanging on by his fingertips. Clerical work, the phrase even now makes his lip curl, remembering the sneer he had for 'office wallahs'. Sat in an open plan floor with plants and partitions, he feels on display, but he's trying. He listens as people come up and give him small talk: – When the kids grow up and leave, the dogs remain. – Marlene from Supplies: she's something. – Drinking the duty free and falling asleep on the beach.

He listens and puzzles and works. Pen always going across paper at his desk, but the sense of it escapes him. He envies the man who bounces past each day, strip of blue sock, light blue shirt, he knows where he's going, has glasses that dim in the light. A man like that is protected, knows the right people, has it worked out. He recognizes the signs.

Everything there is to be done is done by her, thought Mary. Her life is shopping and washing and cooking, looking after. And when she does get time to herself she folds up, slumps.

One night she was sat on the bed and John was looking down at her, scratching his head, and all he'd say was 'Odd, odd, very odd' like a university professor in a sitcom. And 'Don't you think I know? Of course I do.' She caught him looking at his teeth, snapping them, lips back, in the bathroom mirror. Then sometimes he would sound like a pensioner moaning: 'In my day . . .' She didn't know him. Her John had disappeared into this man's physical presence – tall, striking, his smile something like a knife in these dark rooms.

Anything on handicap on telly she watches, but none of them seem to match her son. The doctors don't seem able to tell her much. She visits him in care, taking the bus to the edge of the city, expert now at finding her way through corridors and courtyards, but John has stopped coming.

She looks forward to summer, she leans forward to summer. Wheeling him to the park, down car-lined roads, across dual carriageways. People on buses look out at her. When she got to the park she'd carry on walking. 'Look, look at that,' she'd stop at last and say, and point within sunlit leaves at red wings opening. She'd try to line his eye up with the butterfly, thinking, what's he see? She'd carry on walking the cambered lanes that bent through trees and opened out on to a pond. The odd cyclist would spin by, the odd dog lope, snuffle, sometimes come to the wheels. She read the same graffiti, stood under the same red decaying kite stuck in a tree and only visible in winter. She'd walk and walk, tiring, but could listen to her feet, the wheels, all day.

It was true what her husband said, she had her hair done for his homecoming. This time the man in the styled shirt had a cold, kept coughing into her hair. A dead afternoon, she the only customer, buses drew up outside but no one came in. Comb and scissors then mousse and spray were applied. All the time chat. She watched the new person emerge, her face growing angular in the mirror. Her hair, swirls and clumps of ginger, swept away by a silent girl in pink.

*

The day Mike comes home this time is a hot Wednesday in June. The man who brings him chain smokes, sweats and complains but helps her with the deckchair. He talks swigging Coke, where no talk has been on a weekday and she does not know how to reply.

At work John is nervy, knowing what day it is, is distracted by the people who collect by the drinks machine near his desk. He spends fifteen minutes watching the woman clean out the machine, refill it with lines of white cups, spoons of powder from big tins, deft with it. Keys dangle from her hip.

'Lying on boulders,' Mary says, 'you look as if you're lying on boulders.'

All the back gardens centre on a tall sycamore around which these houses were built. This tree bursts out in birdsong, like a music box set off. Unexpected, as if it's the first time she's heard it.

They watch together (she thinks) the birds fly down to shed roofs to peck at white bread. She comments on the day – See three cats under the hedge? – insects everywhere.

Sweat trickles down from her underarms, but he is shielded by the slatted wooden fence. She notices the bin has started to smell. The heat begins to twist her.

'You used to be noisier.' Then she goes in.

Things whirl for John with the heat, the work and the swish of suits and skirts going by; he needs a drink at lunchtime, in the works bar. He knows no one there, sits alone, grips his drink.

A market researcher calls and Mary lets him in. Young man in a suit, a student doing holiday work. He takes off his jacket, drinks her tea. He holds up cards. 'I find serving real coffee to guests – good, very good, poor.' She leaves him every few minutes to check out the back but doesn't tell him why. When he leaves she sees him out and notices that his short hair turns long at the back. She looks at the strands curled over his collar, she watches them all down the street.

Walking back through the car park, John sees the woman still in her green overall, still with the keys at her hip, open a car door.

'Hi,' he says, waves across.

She looks up.

He explains where he works. 'You did our machine this morning.'

She nods, waits. She is far enough away to see him as attractive and for a minute imagines getting to know him, but becomes impatient when he doesn't speak. She gets in and drives off, threading through the stationary cars, each radiating, air bending above them, and he watches her go, sweat in the creases of his eyelids.

The sun turns the tree's shadow into every garden. Into them also come the few that are home, sunbathers with towels and radios, invisible behind fences, hedges and walls. She touches her recently cropped hair, feels the sun flat and hot as an iron on her face. She's not old, she thinks, she just feels old.

As does John at his desk imagining he got in the car with the caterer and they drove out of the city, up some narrow-laned hill where he fucked her in the back seat, among the cups and catering tins.

His boss, who hasn't talked to him since his first day,

breaks from a party going by to have a word: 'King. John King. Am I right? And how are we getting on?'

'Fine.' He tries to point his beer breath away.

A wind starts, stirs the tree, leaves in their green prime stirring. Behind this the hum and clank of the rush hour, the long, intermittent squeal of air brakes.

'That's a bus,' she tells him.

Father's home, shoes clack down the entry, the back gate's latch clicks up and he is in the yard. Tall man with a smile showing in the darkness of his face, the sun behind him.

'You're here then?' Drink is with him, in his pocket a bottle, in his belly two.

It is a yellow, slanting evening. Mary, her face cut in four by the window frame's shadow, sees him, thinks of first meetings, thinks of his hands on her in the corners of pubs.

'She needs you,' he says, a little sloppy. 'We all need you.' He bends to see Mike's eyes. Flying ants are in the air. 'Even God in His heaven needs you.'

She comes out with food, mixed in a plastic bowl. She says hello, prepared to talk or be silent, sees her husband sway and stands the other side of the deckchair.

The sun falling sends the tree's shadow over Mike's body. His head is the last to go under. Like slipping underwater, she thinks. His head waits patiently, blinking and stern. She puts the spoon to his lips and his eyes swivel upwards. His father looks up too and sees the sky blue with a yellow hole burnt through it and scabbed with cloud.

Taking Doreen out of the Sky

When it was all over I hung about the place to see how the next shift would take it. They mostly knew already and the Friday night clocking-on was even more subdued than usual. Me and George Brackon bandied a few words, said we'd meet at the clubhouse tomorrow. Carry on like it never happened. I watched them form groups, out of their places, some of them absently pulling on half-melted gloves. It was that quiet you could actually hear their voices.

Then I left for the bus. At the shelter I looked up at the firm's logo, the first thing to strike you about that place. Above the big glassed entrance, protruding from the wall, is a model of the globe. Americas one side, Africa and Europe the other (Russia, of course, is buried in the bricks). The equator is a big steel ring with 'We Encompass the

World' printed – indented – on it. FALCON STEEL RINGS LTD is painted round this world, takes up all the earth's atmosphere. At night, as now, they spotlight the whole thing. With the blue of the sea marred by strips of red land it looks like some drunkard's bulbous eye – a bit like Brackon's.

The bus came and I went upstairs, lit a fag and watched that world disappear.

I remembered my first day there, being led by Hawkins through that swanky reception, all lights and phone-girls, to the cathedral-high factory behind. So different from the backstreet hutches made of corrugated iron and breeze block where I'd always worked, when I had a job. Here, once you'd got through the black rubber swing doors, you were confronted with a huge machine almost touching the skylight. Men in oily blue stood at various heights working it. On both sides of the aisle leading there clumps of machinery sprouted within wire grids. Lathe arms, levers, wheels. The noise was like being attacked by an army equipped with tanks and ack-ack guns, the odd shouts and whistles seemed made of tin.

It was a chunk of paradise to me – a big firm with big wages. Falcon's had factories worldwide, steel rings being just one of many products, and they had a reputation for looking after their workers. Here, they had a canteen, they issued you with boots and overalls, they had a generous pension scheme, a complaints procedure, bonuses, overtime available. They even had a resident doctor, for Christ's sake. I was smiling to myself as Hawkeye (as we later knew him) was telling us this at the factory entrance. Three or four years, I reckoned, as we followed our new chargehand's bald patch through the towering maze, three or four years and Doreen would be opening the front door on to the street, perhaps a garden.

The bus stopped and I heard some familiar wheezing coming up the stairs. Eric's face, gone pink and pippy with cold, appeared. He made a beeline for me. He's just retired from Falcon's and wanted to know more about today's news. He asked me who the new boss thought he was.

I shook my head. 'Don' know, Eric, someone out of Oxford I shouldn't wonder.'

'That's it, that's it.' Eric was excited, trembling. 'What do all these college chaps know about it when it comes down to it? I said what do they know when it comes down to it?' His old blue eyes had gone as clear as an adolescent's in that canned-tomato face. Behind his head I saw the city framed in lights – it was just dark enough to see that the Rotunda clock said 17:22.

'When I heard it really done my fruit. What happens, I thought, what happens when they want steel rings again? What happens then?' The Fuji ad lit up green, panel after panel, disappeared into Eric's ear, went out and began again.

'Just no call for steel these days,' I said, ''S all computers now.' I was tired, I didn't want to talk about it. That's why I hadn't caught the works' bus – words wouldn't reverse the closure, not now, words were no good. While Eric rambled on I glanced down at the street below, mainly boarded up shops. Through the leafless branches of a street tree I noticed this man drag something out of a house. It turned out to be a woman, she was kicking, he pulled. Passers-by passed by.

'. . . the Germans, the Japs, the Asians they all patter-nize each other,' Eric was saying, 'but we don't. That's the trouble with this country, you never see a British car abroad.' His thin voice was accompanied by the sound of twigs scraping the dirt-fogged windows.

I got out in the city centre and the air was so cold it was like sucking down glass. Although I'm not yet thirty, the cold seems to hit me harder each year. The city went on regardless – busy with traffic and people and business as night came down fast above the lights – and I too wandered about, despite the cold, didn't want to go home just yet. Because of the closure I suppose, official with today's letter. Nothing new really, nothing unexpected, but all of us were up in arms to find the notice in the wage packet, sneaked in amongst the money it seemed. I thought 'Gordon' Banks, the big ginger lad who started with me, was going to hit Hawkeye, breathing that heavily he was at his chargehand. But we talked him down, out of it. It was hardly Hawkeye's fault.

Hawkeye and Banks have never hit it off, ever since that first day. Hawkeye had proudly taken us through the simple trimming operation – a machine knifed out the ragged middles of rubber seals, hot off the presses. He had brightly warned of the scalpel-sharp blade needed to produce smoothness. He had boasted of the machine's 'delicacy', and its efficiency ('One thousand five hundred a shift!'). He had explained how the seals were sent to be fitted into the steel rings. He then asked if we had any questions, rubbing his hands together as if relishing the prospect. 'Can we smoke at these poxy machines?' Banks asked, with a breath of onion you could smell above the rubber.

And a week or two later, when Hawkeye was rummaging in our boxes in his quest for the perfect seal, Banks said, 'Well I've learnt something, boss.' 'What's that, Gord?' (Hawkeye was very quick to pick up nicknames.) Banks, straightening from his task and rubbing his hands in an imitation of his supervisor, said very seriously, 'It's this what I've learnt. Always shit on the company's time. A golden rule. Always shit on the company's time. Save it up in the mornings.'

No, Hawkeye and Banks have never been the best of mates, but violence was never a possibility until this morning.

I walked down through the arcade, polished wood, marble and posh shops (most of which were closing). I was looking for a pub but the centre's all changed since I did my pubbing in the early seventies. I followed this girl out into the dead middle of this city. Although late November, bits of drained slush in corners, she was dressed for summer and her legs flashed like skinned sticks in the forest of the muffled up crowd. Starlings were swooping down to fill the ledges of buildings, their shrill noise stronger than the traffic. I wondered whether I'd processed as many seals as there were birds in Birmingham in my eighteen months at Falcon's (quite likely, I thought). Each seal supposedly getting us a ha'penny or so nearer the ground. I worry about Doreen cooped up with Ian inside that flat. Though she hardly complains, I can see her tightening with it; it's getting to her insides, making her ill.

I got stopped on the corner of New Street by this smiling character, a Steve Davis lookalike. He gave me a leaflet

which said 'Are You Upward Bound?' next to a shaky
drawing of a rocket taking off. With the crowd jostling us
he tried to give me the chat about God. I was having none
of it. 'In a hurry,' I said, but I did glance through the leaflet
as I walked off. 'PLAIN FACTS concerning your FUTURE'
it said inside. 'Either you are on the DOWNWARD course
which leads to destruction or on the UPWARD path which
leads to life.' I looked for the organization – 'The Christ
Mission. Coming Shortly to Your City – Malcolm Sales.' Of
course, all those posters with that man's toothy face.
American evangelist staring at you from buses and hoard-
ings. Everywhere in the city. I pocketed the leaflet, figuring
me and Doreen could have a giggle over it later.

I went into a phone box to ring Doreen and remembered, as I listened to our phone ring four miles away, how
she broke her news to me three years ago in a hot summer.
We were lying on that slope of the Lickeys that gives such
a grandstand view of Birmingham. Half the city seemed to
be up there in bikinis or bare chests running about or taking it easy like us. It reminded me of a painting I'd seen on
a jigsaw box of Doreen's made up of brightly coloured dots
of people in a park, only they wore more clothes in those
days. It was so hot the air was unclear, things were shimmering. Doreen had her legs on show to brown them, her
skirt hitched right up. I watched a kite soar, a tiny red slash
in the sky, as she said that a baby was coming, was on its
way. We lay between the blue and the green going through
names. The city, far below us, seemed a strange, mysterious place in its dusty heat haze, like some technological
Stonehenge.

I told Doreen I'd be home late and she said OK as if it

was something I do every night which it isn't. In the background I heard the jaunty tune of the *Six O'Clock News*, and Ian's half sentences ('Mummy wants cleaning,' I thought I heard). I waited for more and eventually she said, 'About an hour then?' I felt her – what shall I say? – her pull through the wire and half regretted not going straight home. Instead I went straight into the Train, which I'd seen opening from the phone box.

From the outside the pub is painted to look like a carriage. It's right in the centre and I pass it every day on my way to the real train, but this was the first time I'd been inside. It was done out like a train: the seats were the same shape and the same dirty tartan and had string racks above. I used to like trains, before I started to use them regular.

'Not exactly 'ot is it?' said the barmaid as she pulled my beer. She was black; in a white blouse she looked blacker.

'Certainly isn't. 'Sno joke this weather,' but I smiled anyway. She filled the pint.

'You the first-in-last-out type or just a quickie on the way home?'

'Just a quickie.'

'Thought so.'

As I took my drink and sat by the window (this too like a train's with arrows showing how far you could open before getting a draught), I thought, am I that easy to spot? It's true I'm not much of a drinker now, not much of one, not like I used to be. Me and Doreen sometimes travel out to the firm's social of a Saturday (as we will tomorrow, babysitter permitting). We drink while a local pop group plays. I sit and watch the massed Falcon faces, bored or laughing, drunk or getting there, up with their partners for their Saturday night dance. Some of the women, solid arms bared in their going-out dresses, dance with fisted hands pumping as if they were kneading dough. Doreen and me sometimes have a twirl, but not if I can help it. I feel a prat: there might be someone like me watching from the Formica-top tables edging the dance area. When I'm dancing I feel I'm doing something peculiar, something insane, and the three minutes drag by . . . unless I'm the worse for wear and can bury myself in Doreen for an end of evening smooch. I like to get my face next to hers, taste her secrets in that flat patch of flesh behind her ear.

Usually we sit out the night with George Brackon and his wife – they're old friends of Doreen's family. Banks sometimes joins us but the Brackons don't really approve of him. I suppose I shouldn't either but we have this special link because we started on the same day. He's a clown, of the old type. He drinks and shows us his tattoos, boos the pop group, makes pyramids of half-full glasses and gets thrown out a lot. One night he dropped his trousers and set light to one of his notorious farts as a comment on Falcon's management. He puts his arm round Doreen and tells her silly jokes – What do you call a fast cake? Scone – until she smiles. I wait with him for that slow grey grin of hers, it's worth waiting for, her face loses a few years and those eyes melt to chocolate.

But as I say the Brackons don't approve, and usually we make a foursome. George sits comfortable in his Arran cardigan tucking pints into an ample belly, smelling of cigars and aftershave. He always exhales through his nose as he drinks, so that his glass is half full of smoke. I notice these things because I get a bit bored to tell the truth; the

only thing we have in common is we're both Albion fans.
His wife's quiet, normally good humoured, but sometimes
she has outbursts of spleen (I think that's the right word)
that tighten her face like a screw. I used to wonder if me
and Doreen would end up like these two, sat in the club
Saturday after Saturday. Don't get me wrong, we've had
some good times there, it's just George's drink-shot,
Falcon-emblem eyes that worry me. That and the belly that
looks as if he's swallowed the football he's always on
about. And is it possible that Doreen could end up as
lemony, as tight faced as Mrs Brackon sometimes is? Only
last week I happened to mention Longdon, our shop stew-
ard, to George and she turned on me. Her glasses reflected
the strip lighting behind the bar (I saw little figures move
in there) as she scowled. 'Makes me think of Moscow that
man does,' and she shivered in her white frilled dress.

I was shivering myself in the Train: there was no heating
on that I could detect and the beer had cooled my insides.
I drank up, waved to the barmaid, and left for the 6.45.

In the Bull Ring they already had Christmas music lul-
labying the last few commuters. I made my way through
the hoop-hatted Rastas at the top of the escalator and
descended smoothly downwards.

I only just made it and had to get in a non-smoker. I sat
on my hands and tried not to think about it. I watched this
upright bloke in a suit calculate figures in a folder balanced
on his knees. Across the aisle this girl sat back, her eyes far
away. That's how I like to think of Doreen. Daydreaming.
When her face smooths out, when she lets the world roll
over. Like cats do on hot days. I like to watch her come out
of it, slowly. At work when my body goes through its

repetitive motions and the noise hums my brain to nothing, when I'm about as bored as you can get, I like to picture her like that. Sat at home, Ian fast in a nap, Dionne Warwick singing low on the player and Doreen sipping at a fag, daydreaming.

I realized I was staring at this girl, she had gone red-cheeked, so for the rest of the journey I looked out of the window. The train hurtled beneath towerblocks and the lit windows, coloured squares, looked like a game being played right across the city. We fled over dual carriage-ways where fleets of cars came and went, their eyes and tails alight. All those cars – somewhere buried in their engines, vitally, are a few steel rings, perhaps some that I've handled. They go into Concorde Falcon's rings do, they go into this train I'm sitting in. But not any more, not any longer.

At the station someone had scrawled 'You Are Now Entering a Job Free Zone' which made me smile a bit.

It was trying to snow. I walked past our crumbling local ('Hot Pies' in black felt tip), the secondhand furniture shop ('DHSS Grants Accepted' in red felt tip) and over the bridge. The two still canals had lamplight smeared on them. I had to wait while turbanned men, sleek with black beards, loaded a van with polythened clothes from their factory, a converted cinema. Steam came out of ducts at the side. I watched a group of women in gaudy saris clock off, pulling on anoraks and gabbling in their horse-swift language. They stood in the light spilling out of the double doors and I saw hair, lips, jewels and eyes catch that radiance. They seemed to sparkle in the damp night.

I thought Doreen might be looking down at me – perhaps bringing in washing from that oversized flowerbox which is our balcony – but I didn't check as I turned into our block.

I'd seen Peacock Towers go up when I was a kid, I haven't always lived there. (Named not after the bird but one of the councillors who commissioned them.) Ever since, people have been queuing to get out. With only one kid we're a long way down the list. (Ken Saunders, who used to live above us, said that that and the tax were the only reason he had six.)

I hesitated outside our door, wheezing like Eric from the eight flights of stairs and the smell of piss. I gave one of our neighbours a smile. She went past in fur-collared coat and old-fashioned knee-length boots, heading for the lift, muttering. I could have told her the lift was out of order but didn't, just watched her press the button and wait. I pressed our button and waited. I wanted to see Doreen open up but it was the lad from the flat below who answered. He's got these flowerpot-red eyebrows that are two arches above his glasses and I noticed these first. My smile-for-Doreen left my face. All my tiredness came in a rush, I felt tipsy with it.

'Come in,' he said. 'Doreen's just putting the kid to bed.'

'Right,' I said, pushing past. I was curt to him for a bit but I knew he wouldn't get the hint. He was a young man with plans and thought everybody was interested in them.

I left him in the kitchen and went in to see Doreen and Ian. Doreen had just got him to sleep and shushed me over her shoulder. I watched her turn about, in sweater and skirt, like a video in slow motion, finger to her lips. Her face is so familiar to me, I have watched the freckles fade and merge to give her that colour of cake, slightly under-baked. Her eyes range in colour, depending on her mood, from giraffe-blob brown to almost black. Now they moved like two pennies in their slots as they searched my face. I could tell she knew, though she said nothing.

We never kiss when we first meet, which is odd, I suppose, after four years. It's as if we have to get to know each other again each night. We stood looking down at Ian, oblivious in a fat sleep. Against the white of the pillow I noticed her zip tag stuck out of her skirt at the hip and I thought of her legs stood in the mesh of tights beneath.

'Get rid of Joe,' I hissed as we came out. That surprised her, and me.

But first we had to listen to the young man's plans again. We drank tea out of mugs in the living room. The telly was on low – a documentary, there were tanks on the screen. Joe had just started as a salesman and had his future all worked out, planned like a picnic, how his wages would go up – salary he called it – his position. His thoughts worked themselves out on his cheerful face, decorated with tinted glasses and a first-growth moustache. Like everybody else he was only in Peacock Towers for a short time, he'd be out soon.

'When the commission starts rolling in. There's real money to be made, door to door. You get the right techniques and people will buy anything. You just have to present it in the right way. The company gives you training.'

'What if people don't want the stuff?' asked Doreen.

'There's ways and means.' His lip curled as if he was winking behind those brown-tinted glasses. 'There's ways and means. I'm optimistic, I am. With the right techniques.'

He liked the sound of that word and repeated it, 'Techniques.'

'But isn't it wrong? I mean pressurizing some old dear out of her pension.'

Joe looked like he'd never considered this. 'I don't see it that way,' he said. He wouldn't. I thought of what Banks would say to him, he would have a go, but I couldn't be bothered. I left them to it, got up and stared at the massive gallery of windows in the block opposite. Those with curtains open showed scenes like ours – people grouped round TVs. I sometimes imagine the whole front being swung open on hinges, to reveal families in their sets of clapboard boxes, like those cages of rats you see in animal experiments on telly. I can just see some big hand coming in, picking on someone, putting them through tests.

I kept glancing back at Doreen leaning forward in her seat, listening, gently arguing her point. She was her usual self; the world could come to Doreen and she'd try and make room. I pictured her on a beach – we'd planned to go to Spain next summer – I kept thinking of that. Being there.

In a patch of silence in which you could hear the aquarium bubbling (fish are allowed pets in the Towers), Doreen nagged me with her eyes to say something. I could only think of, 'Met Ma Yates on the stairs. Now there's a character.'

'Dog rough she is,' Joe snapped in, 'nasty as a nailfile.'

Doreen protested that she wasn't as bad as all that but Joe said we didn't know her like he did. 'You 'ant 'ad 'er soliciting at your door.'

At last he went and Doreen's visitor smile relaxed, small lines showing where it had been. She asked me why I was late. 'Well I gathered you hadn't won the pools when you didn't come home in a taxi.' She told me to go and eat. 'I did you burgers but they all stuck together, I couldn't get them apart.' I pictured her fingernails, which she is trying to grow, prising at the frozen meat.

I ate the warmed up dinner alone in the kitchen looking out over the clumps and cranes of the city, dotted with lights like a jumble of grounded ships. My reflection hung like a ghost over the scene.

I was thinking of Falcon's, all that space going to waste, the buildings boarded up. No more fleeing the place at 4.30, or limping back in the mornings. No more clocking on. Falcon's would end up like the old tyre place a mile down the road, just the remains of a factory, a massive ribcage of girders dissolving in the rain.

One of Ian's pictures was Sellotaped to the fridge door. Three crayoned lines – could be a waxy hand, a bush, a TV aerial. I thought that when he's older, my age, he will be in a different world and will wonder at all this fuss over steel and factory. But I try not to think of his future, don't want to burden him with other people's ambitions. My mother did that to me, pushing me through CSEs, and look where it got me. When I turned out just like Dad I could almost taste her disappointment, like tea leaves on the tongue. My idea about Ian is to wait and see . . . but it's hard, Doreen is already picking out some vaguely professional future for him. She's been talking to my mother.

I went in, swallowing the last of the food. On telly the BBC world was busily feeding on itself. I told Doreen the factory was closing down. She said she'd read about it in the evening paper.

'What'll we do now?' she wanted to know. I shrugged, what can you say?

'We'll get by,' is what I did say and laid my arm round her shoulders. She let it lie. She gripped my hand once, then concentrated on the film that was just starting. I did the same for a while but I was so worn out I couldn't tell you what it was about. All I remember is American accents and lots of fake blood which looked even more artificial, pulsing, because our colour balance is up the chute.

We talked a bit. I asked how Ian had been ('Bombing around as usual'), if she'd been out (no – the lift was out of order). We had a bit of a barney about Joe who I put down as a money grabber, but Doreen thought I was too harsh.

'If you'd trained for something instead of drinking away your youth perhaps we wouldn't be here now,' she started and there was no answer to that. She let it drop but what she'd said seemed to hang about the room.

We both lit cigarettes, smoked together, shifted apart. We sat under our individual strings of smoke. The fish in the aquarium gawped at us.

About eleven I had a real urge for her and flicked the hair from her cheek, as if removing ash or something, getting closer to her. Her hair had the smell of apples (the new shampoo on the bath's corner, not yet stuck there by wasp-yellow drippings).

I said, 'Who's your favourite television personality?' There was an award show on and I used this to start a conversation. I wanted to get round to the question, I wanted to hear yes, but I wasn't sure how.

Doreen, head down, fiddled with her wedding ring, but

only managed to twist her finger (she has put on a little weight since Ian).

'Why is it closing then?' Eyes still on her hands.

'How should I know?' But I added when she looked up, 'It's this new bloke, new boss, brought in by the firm. He's streamlining.'

Doreen waited. When I didn't go on she said, 'Streamlining?' as if I'd made up the word.

'Yes, you know, cutting down, the non-profit bits.' Then I said defensively, ''S not my fault.'

'But don't people still want steel rings?'

'Don't look like it. What's it say in the paper?'

'What happened then, at work?'

I sighed. 'Well there was meetings. Hawkeye took it bad' – he did, he looked like an aged and constipated Bobby Charlton; 'old "Gordon" threw a wobbly at him, near enough hit him.'

She nodded.

'A bloke from the firm came to explain the whys and the wherefores; a catalogue man, tie and everything. Very symp-a-thet-ic he was, oh yes, could see he had another job lined up.'

'What are the whys and wherefores?'

'Oh profit and that, percentages, trouble with raw materials, I couldn't follow all of it.'

'And that's it then is it? Just like that you're out of a job,' she added – 'again.'

She didn't say 'and we're stuck here', but that's what she meant. I said, 'Happens all the time, love. What's it say in the paper?'

'Not much.'

'Gis a look.' I was glad to turn away from those eyes, which looked both defeated and angry, going black and wet. I turned to the paper; the story was on the front page, near the bottom, under the headline '800 JOBS TO GO'.

'We got a letter,' I said and reached for my coat hanging on the arm of the sofa. The Jesus leaflet came out with the letter.

'Oh read that. 'S dead funny. Malcolm Sales's lot.'
'Who?'

'You know. The evangelist, buckets of blood for sinners. On at the Villa.'

I left her reading and went to make coffee. I poked my head in to see Ian but in the gloom I could only make out the MFI chest of drawers covered in stickers. I tiptoed in and bent to kiss the dark sweat-smudged curls, a baby taste still, strange in the coloured darkness. A pure, warm taste, not wrecked yet like adults were with stuff, drink, drugs, dirt. It came to me in that room, my eyes gradually picking out toys and story books and cartoon wallpaper, it came to me that our marriage was like that: in its infancy, not wrecked yet. Whatever might happen it was not wrecked yet.

I listened to him sleeping until I calculated the kettle had boiled. At least I'll see more of him, I thought as I went back along the narrow corridor. Perhaps I'll stay with him while Doreen goes back to the supermarket, if she wants to, if they'll have her back.

I went in with the mugs to be greeted by laughter. Not Doreen's, some celebrity had cracked a joke in his acceptance speech. Doreen was reading the leaflet, the firm's letter lay on the arm and I picked it up and read it again, perhaps for the fifth time. All the time I kept glancing across at Doreen, trying to gauge her mood, but she kept her head down.

Then she asked, 'Well, are we upward or downward bound?'

'God knows,' I said and laughed for the first time today. 'Downward, let's hope, out of this flat.'

We drank up and went to bed. I missed Doreen's undressing: she was already in bed, sheets tight across her breasts, reading a library book when I came in from the bathroom.

We lay separately, Doreen slightly frowning at her book. The woman next door was singing, snatches of la-las, words, the song of a mother. Some nights there's screaming and fights, locked out husbands banging on doors, or loud parties, but tonight there was just the woman singing and the patter of drizzle. I felt the Falcon rhythm, 1,500 movements a day, loosen and dissolve.

Doreen turned on her side with the book. The bed-clothes shifted and I saw a large area of her back – the dark hair fell at an angle across her neck and one shoulder. The other shoulder blade made a deep triangular shadow, it looked like the root of a wing. She seemed as exotic as an Asian curled next to me. I thought of holidays, of small waves being doused in the sand. Her ear was pricked, I could tell, for a move from me or perhaps Ian's bubbling cry. She put the book down, leaned to switch out the lamp.

'We will get out of here, Mark, won't we?' She said it mildly, I couldn't be sure she'd spoken. She didn't turn round.

The woman next door was still singing. In the dark

Doreen's back had turned grey, it almost seemed to be transmitting like a television left on after closedown. I thought of all the days she'd lived that had brought her to this point, lying in bed beside me.

Then I stopped thinking, slotted into her curl until I felt contact along my whole length, my arm beneath hers round the waist. She had a grassy smell of talc and babies. I had her tight and felt her warmth enter and spread in me. 'Doreen, Doreen,' I was saying before I knew it, chanting it softly like a song, 'Doreen, Doreen.'

Nothing Personal

When I bought the house the floorboards were rotting and I had to pull them up. They stayed up for weeks, then months. Finally I sold them at a timberyard round the corner. I couldn't get used to seeing the gritty rubble, a foot down, when I came in or went out.

I've sold most things off: the three-piece, the stereo, the refrigerator. All I've got now is in the one room upstairs, around the mattress. You don't need much: a change of clothes, a chair, a kettle. Burglars would be sorry they bothered; nevertheless I listen for them. I'm sure they have broken in, just looked round and left, but I never find a footprint or a forced door.

One Saturday I put all my remaining tapes, the bust tape recorder, some books I found in the attic and my spare pair of shoes in a box and carried it downstairs. It was tricky getting out, I had to walk along the edge, the last floorboard, to the front door.

'Selling up?' It was the bloke from two doors down with the dog and the belly. He strokes one as much as the other.

I nodded, let him poke at items in my box.

'Heard the latest?' he said. Besides Izzy, he's the only one who talks to me around here. He usually goes on about sport and 'kids in the street'. 'They're going to demolish it all. Council's been round.'

At this point some kids in a wheelchair, HOSPITAL PROPERTY clearly stamped on it, charged up and down deliberately falling out and doing wheelies. It made the dog yap and we had to step in the road.

He started, like a bloke from a comic with his fist raised, 'Bloody kids,' and I was off.

In the secondhand shop I got ten quid although I asked for fifteen. Luckily the owner didn't try the recorder which looked quite smart.

I bought some tobacco, put the fiver in my back pocket, the change in my front and the three pound coins on the counter of the bookie's. I chose an outsider, the best odds I could find in the next race, and it came up. I only half listened to the results come through on the crackling system, and when I collected the money, over £40, I somehow felt it was my due.

It was only when I got outside the place, two converted terrace houses with crude sporting pictures in the window, that the money felt warm in my pocket.

Izzy followed me out. I should have noticed him lurking

in some corner or another. I did owe him some baccy so we went to the nearest pub, a Sikh place – turbanned heads nodding to the Asian music on the juke box – and had a couple. A bloke tried to sell us watches and furry toys out of a suitcase. Izzy was going on about this job he had lined up, he'd been round the factories that were still operating, one of them thought they could fit him in.

'There ain't nothing to it,' he said, pulling an imaginary lever up and down. 'Anyone could do it, man, woman or beast.'

Then he tried to touch me for some of the winnings. I said no, I was going to blow it by myself, away from here.

After that I finished my pint and got up. Izzy, who's half black, fingered day-old stubble and watched me get to the door before jumping up and coming after me. I walked fast, past the shunting yards, along the canal, I ran to traffic islands, lorries roaring at my back, but still he kept up.

'Don't you trust me? In a week I'll have a wage packet.'

I reminded him of the week in hand.

He tried to slow us down when we got near pubs and finally I gave him a fiver and he dropped off at one of them.

'You won't regret it,' he said.

Only then did I look about me. I thought I'd head for town which I could see, little towers at the foot of the broad road. But I saw the football crowd, a surge of bobbing bodies, squeezing out of the side roads halfway down. I turned and went the other way.

After streets and streets of terraces, I turned off through

a gloomy, open park and came out the other side on to a housing estate. Sixties job, four storeys, flats with peeling white woodwork. I walked until I found a pub, the Blue Ox I think it was. On an apron of concrete with bollards. Kids sat smoking, planning mischief. Low building, pebble dash. I went down the long corridor. Two men were arguing, a boy between them.

'Yes, Martin, your dad went out with my missus.'

'I didn't.'

'You telling me you didn't? Fucking cheek of it.'

'When?'

'You know when.'

'You mean last Friday. That wasn't going out.'

They'd said all that by the time I'd got to them and they didn't look at me as I went past.

I stood at the bar and finished my first pint quickly; all that walking had made me thirsty. Ordered another. The barman was Scottish.

I took my third drink to a seat by the frosted window and watched smudges, people, approach. I slouched back, crossed my feet like a regular, feeling the alcohol take effect.

The place soon started to fill up. The noise level increased. The pool table was activated by 50ps, the light came on over a cracked dartboard.

Everyone seemed to know each other, shouting greetings.

'Are you getting enough exercise?' Someone near the pool table.

'It. He means it – is it getting enough exercise?' from across the room.

Two women, sisters I thought, sat near by. They were dressed up, one in yellow, one in red, freckled cleavage on show. Their men brought them half lagers and I watched them settle and look at the territory they were making with their drinks put down, packets of fags.

One of the women looked a bit like my first 'serious' girlfriend, Tricia. She was something – blonde, fat legs and a smooth, elegant face. She smoked Consulate out of the side of her mouth, called me 'soldier'. We lasted almost a year. I had money then, left to me by my dad, and we both gave up work and lived off it. A grand time.

There were others, but none of them lasted even that long. There was Jan, a chocolate fiend ('food of the Gods', she used to say), but it didn't show on her. Thin as string. She wore a lot of red I remember – belts, handbags, shoes. Then there was Carmen, who changed her name by deed poll and liked communal living so much she tried to introduce another boyfriend into the household. Carol, Jill. They'd all move in with me, get themselves organized and leave within four months. I used to wonder about that – four months – was it some kind of cycle, a menstrual season?

I was deep into thinking about this when I was joined by two men. I got into a round with them. One – short prickles of hair round his balding head, fifty if he was a day, said he was an ex-wrestler – showed me his scars, said he had a bit of rubber in his knee. He demonstrated its flexibility and pretended he couldn't stop his leg swinging. He was a small man but with plenty of tattooed muscle on show under his shirt sleeves. The other was his sidekick, a large man who backed up his pal – 'It's true, it's true.' They had some in-joke about the Flintstones, called each other Barney and Fred. I heard all about Barney, the wrestler's exploits with women fans. He said he had a collection of knickers at home that had been thrown into the ring during bouts.

I told them I was a sandblaster, which I was once. I was surprised how the details of that long ago job came back to me. Putting my arms in the gloves hanging in the glass case. The whip of the tube as I thumbpressed the nozzle. The shine coming on the metal.

They tried to get me to play cards with them but I refused. I knew they'd try to fleece me, working as a double act. I was careful not to show any money when I got a round in. They insisted on a game. A pack was produced and Barney dealt. Page Three girls, grimy and biroed, slid through the beer to me. Obviously marked.

'No thanks,' I said. I said I was just off, on my way somewhere, and made a show of getting my things together.

There was some kind of do going on in the back room. I wondered if I couldn't just slip in. The money could keep for another night. My last chance of anything, I felt, would be this party.

I joined in the toasts, the cheers and the more general gestures. It was a twenty-first. The boy was goofy, a bit pissed. He thanked everyone with his arm round a short, fattish girl who grinned up at him.

'And let's hear it for Mum,' he said after some prompting, and the woman in yellow from the bar was pushed forward. She pointed out the food available. I loaded up the paper plate. I hadn't eaten all day.

When the music started I looked for the mother or her sister but they were at the centre of a crowd of relatives. An old biddy asked me to dance. Her eyes leaked from the pupils. She called me Mike. She grinned the whole time and stood apart, shifting from foot to foot. She held her hands to her ears when the crescendo began. She gave me a peck on the cheek, a squeeze of the arm, said, 'You be a good boy then, Mike.' 'I will,' I said.

About 11.30 I left, nothing much doing. I stopped in the doorway to light a fag. There was a motorbike by the pavement, lad on it in fringed leather kissing a girl who stood by. He was stroking her thin, bare legs. I looked, remembering Jan. He broke off. A mean face, pointing out at me from under the hair.

I moved away.

I'd left the estate and was into a grander part of the city, although run down, when I saw them on a corner. Three women bobbing down to look into cars as they went past. By the time I'd reached them, one, the one I fancied naturally, had got into a car. The driver lurched off as if eager to begin.

'Business good?' I said as I got closer. 'Use some more?'

They looked me up and down.

'Where's your car?'

'I'm on foot tonight.'

They laughed. 'Piss off then.'

Another car drew up, an arm out the window, pointing at one, and I was left with the other.

She had a small head inside the mass of backcombed hair. She had a mac which she pulled over her miniskirt.

She looked like she didn't eat enough. Her cheekbones cast pointed shadows down her face. I had a picture of her weighed down with the week's shopping, shuffling home to an out-of-work husband. I never found out what colour her eyes were. Darkish.

'Do you know somewhere we can go?'

She was reluctant, ignored me, scanned for cars. None came. I repeated my question.

'How much you got?'

'Enough.'

'I'm not as cheap as some.'

'Don't be put off by my appearance,' I said. 'I've had a lucky day.' It was the first time I'd actually told someone.

She suggested behind the wall she stood against but I didn't want that.

'There must be somewhere you know.'

There was. We walked off together down the road. I wanted to put my arm round her. Except for Trish none of the women I'd been with went in much for holding hands in the street. A police car slowed and she wrapped her coat round her and put her arm through mine.

'If they ask you're my boyfriend.'

So we did hold each other. I was a bit unsteady from the drink and our hips and thighs bumped together. Burrs of feeling stuck down my side.

'How long have you been doing this?'

'Mind your nose.'

We turned into a cul-de-sac. The large houses you could only glimpse through trees and bushes. I realized most of them were empty, boarded up. She led me through a gate, along a path strewn with rubble. Cans glinted in the over-grown garden.

'What's your name?'

She didn't answer.

'Can I call you something?'

'What?'

'Trish.' Though she was more like Jan.

'If you have to.'

We picked our way on a path that was a thin line between the wall of the house and the shoulder-high bushes. I was scratched by brambles and stumbled a few times, following her skinny figure. We ended up at the back of the house, and stepped in over a kicked down door. I could hardly see her. I stepped on her foot.

'Stay still,' she said. She was listening to make sure nobody else was there. Then she got two candles from somewhere. One she put down, the other she carried.

It was a kitchen, the frames of old units still in place. Graffiti everywhere. Tag names, football teams, obscene drawings. There was soot up the wall and the remains of a fire in one corner.

'Bring the candle.'

She led me to another room. There the floor had been cleared, all the rubbish in one corner, bricks and cans and soiled clothing. A mattress at one end looked chewed by rats. She covered it with her coat.

I tried to kiss her but she turned her face away. I took hold of her breasts and squeezed them like a boy on his first date.

'Trish.'

'What?'

Impatiently she pushed me back and got to her knees, undid my jeans.

'Let me help,' I said, thinking to take my shoes off.

'No need.' She had my cock in her hand. 'Stay still.'

She rolled on a rubber I hadn't seen her get ready. I was going to make a joke about safe sex but she said, 'The appliance of science.' She was broad Brummie.

She lay back on her coat and removed her knickers, which she held the whole time balled in her hand. In the flickering light I saw the dark pubic hair. I started to push down my jeans but she said don't.

'Just get on top of me.'

My heart was beating too fast – the drink. I couldn't control it. It was over almost as soon as I'd entered her.

'Good,' she said, 'that's a relief.'

I made sure I got a touch of her though as I lay spent, on the wane. I let my fingers curl under her thighs. Her pubic hair felt like old tobacco left in a tin. I stroked at her breasts and belly, still within the blouse. I was propped on an elbow.

'Chuck us a fag,' she said. 'In the pocket.' She made me my one concession: 'Till I've smoked this.'

My fingers learnt the shape of her, which I memorized for future reference. She was a bony one. She looked away the whole time.

When I touched her neck she said, 'All right, that's enough.'

She held me to make sure the rubber didn't come off and got out from underneath me.

'That'll be twenty.'

'Ten.'

'I thought you said you were flush.'

'Fifteen then.'

'Twenty.' She was straightening her clothing, picking off bits, stubbing her fag. 'I've got to pay me poll tax.'

She settled for fifteen and whatever change I had.

We left the shell, came back through the garden. I saw the house was tiered like a cake with balconies. We stood at the gate a moment, looked past each other, back at the house, hidden again amongst trees and undergrowth.

I asked her advice on the way home, naming a district next to mine, I don't know why. She directed me back through the 'Blue Ox' estate.

At the mouth of the cul-de-sac she went the other way. Today had been all walking away, I thought.

I entered the estate at another point, through garages and shops with iron shutters down. It hadn't been quite what I'd had in mind, I was thinking, but it had been something of an evening.

They called each other Barney and Fred but I'd known who they were when I passed the bus stop, caught movement and heard the thwack of the spade before I felt it. It hit the back of my knees. As I crumpled forward the brick came down on my head. My face hit the pavement and another blow to the head came down. Then they rolled me over, searched me thoroughly. They were very practised.

'Yabadabadoo,' said Fred on finding my remaining money. But they were disappointed with the haul. I had no watch, no wallet, my clothes were worthless. They made do with the crumpled banknotes.

As the big one got up he kicked out. Luckily he missed my privates.

'Nothing personal,' he said.

I limped through the city streets, following road signs to areas I knew. I was only about four and a half miles from home. Not many about, a few revellers, thieves. At one or two points, by the park, outside a hospital, I thought I wouldn't be able to go on. I considered going into the hospital but decided against it. Too much to explain. When people did go by I straightened up, as best I could.

I realized a railway line I'd passed would lead me directly home, cutting a good half mile from the journey. I turned back. It was a mistake. First of all I had to climb a fence to get on to the track and then the narrow cinder path would disappear under outcrops of weeds or stones slipped from the track. I tried the sleepers but they were too far apart for me. When the line started to vibrate I stood back. Mainly goods trains, trucks with their doors shut, one after the other. A passenger train was a lit streak, out of sight in seconds.

I was never so glad to see our street. I could see my roof from way off. Nearer I saw a tile slide, lodge in the gutter. How many days before the rain soaked through the ceiling? I could move into the back room.

I knew where the embankment was less steep and came down around the old Heineken billboard to the pavement almost opposite my door.

There was a note sticking out of my letterbox. It said:

Met 2 girls. Be at the Railway till 11. Izzy.

I got through the front door with difficulty. I wasn't sure if the door was sticking or my strength had gone completely. I fell to my knees in the dirt, forgetting the drop, and carried forward, face into the stones. I lay there a long time thinking about getting upstairs.

Country Life

The firm wanted me to move to their green-field site, sixty miles south of Birmingham. I talked to Gail about commuting, but then they offered us a house down there, a new one, very favourable terms. That was it for Gail, she'd always liked the idea of country living, and on visits she'd been impressed by the two rivers, the black-beamed buildings, and the Saturday market. There was talk of babies too, and Gail thought the countryside offered a better family environment than bricks, roads and towerblocks. It was decided I'd move down, while she stayed in the city seeing through the house sale. Within two weeks of arriving I'd become involved with a local woman off the assembly line.

Julie had two kids already, been married some time. She told me about her husband right off. He'd converted on her

– 'A born again,' she said. 'Every subject's fucking Jesus.'

We were in the canteen, I'd sat with her. An empty space, blonde company. But she did all the talking. Some people looked up, saw who it was, went back to their trays.

'What I say is if God's so good why'd He make the devil? He made evil. He invented it. What's the point in that?'

'You seem a very serious person,' I said. 'I'm sure you're right.'

'You're a Brummie,' she said. She had the local accent, slow and loping. She asked me what I was doing; I told her about the job. I got lost in some of the details of the software I was developing. On the word 'efficiency' she cut across me –

'Does it mean lost jobs?'

'Oh.' I hadn't thought of that. 'No.'

'Doesn't bother me anyway. Hate this stupid place.'

She looked around the room, checkered with squares of sun from the skylights. Her face was white against the green bank of huge-leaved, plastic plants behind her; it was smooth, bland almost, like a teenager's is, half formed, though you could see she was older – a fair bit older – than that.

'You were saying, about your husband?'

She wasn't reluctant to tell. In twenty minutes she'd told me about her husband's childhood and youth. He hadn't always been like that, she'd known him a long time. He was always a bit of a lad, a bit of a biker. 'Good for a laugh,' she said.

Later that day I happened to look out, bored by a recurring problem in the program, and I saw her on the line. She wore a soft blue cap for work, hair tied back in a pony tail. She turned and swung her head up. Saw me.

We met round the back of the factory, arranging a time when there wouldn't be anybody about. We sat on sacks amongst empty pallets, a skip full of swarf. You could see the river slouching along at the bottom of a field. It was late spring, warmish, and she had bare legs. Through a vent above our heads we heard the shouts, whistles, clang and rumble inside. The air was milky with the smoke and flakes of ash from another factory. She crossed her legs and I could see the pattern of the sack on her thigh. We hardly said a word. We hardly undressed. We did it quickly, scared of someone coming, and when it was over we sprang apart as if someone had.

After a day of air conditioning and screen watching, inputting data, the countryside came as a shock. Julie told her husband she was working overtime and I drove her down country lanes, pulled up by a five-bar gate; looking through it was like opening an Enid Blyton, the field sloping down to the brook, willow trees, the hills behind. We returned again and again. There was somewhere else we went which I can't find now, driving around with Gail. Julie had directed me: through lanes that rose up a hill until they petered out into mud tracks. A walk through a coppice, and at the end, round a corner, a cliff face glittering. An old quarry, the rock scraped into flatness, clumsy facets, at angles. At the foot a pool so blue it looked poisonous.

A few times we went to the new house, sparsely furnished. There was a bed but we would lie about the carpeted rooms, half dressed. Although she only stayed an hour or so, checking her watch, time seemed to slow for me like those summer days of childhood when I would dawdle in the long green stretch of Cannon Hill Park, or be absorbed for hours on deserted Sunday building sites. This had something to do with the silence – I seemed to be the only resident in the small development. Some of the pavements were still gravel. We arrived from the factory as the workmen were leaving. Inside we never put on the TV or radio, we didn't make food. I drank, she smoked. After a while I smoked too.

She still talked about her husband; it was our mutual subject. Every day I'd hear another detail.

'Once he cut himself and I said "OK?" and he went on about healing. That's the way he talks now – "You can't pluck a grape from a thorn bush."'

I didn't realize how serious it was until one night back in the city I was coming out of a cinema with Gail. She was just in front, I could see the white of her neck through the strands of her short haircut. I put my hand on her shoulder, she turned her ear to me, people moved about us.

'There's someone else,' I said so softly it hardly left my mouth. She looked round fully now, her neck creased under her jaw, her eyebrows up – pardon?

'Funny being someone else.'

'What?' Gail frowned now.

I pointed to the 007 poster above the exit: 'The new James Bond.'

Once Julie and I had a sick day and I drove to the town where she lived, ten miles downriver. An upmarket country town – a Promenade with trees, as well as a High Street. I remembered visiting it as a kid, with my mother, on a 'treat' day, shopping in department stores, carpets and lifts, bags bulging by the time we got back to the station, strangely far out of town. But Julie lived in terraces tucked out of sight.

We did the usual things: park, pub meal, the Abbey.

'My husband hates these places,' she said, looking up at the high stained-glass windows. 'Ornament and privilege, he says.'

Organ music began sounding throughout the building: the organist practising. Julie was wearing a dress and looked small in a way she didn't in the factory.

'Come and live with me,' I said, with a nervous laugh. Since the cinema incident I'd been planning this.

She didn't want to know.

'You're not the one,' she said, 'don't think you are.'

After that we were together less and less. Once more by that quarry, in some woods near by. Old leaves and twigs crackled under the coats we laid down. Once in the house. I took what I could get. Less and less.

I was still sleeping with Gail of course. One weekend she came down and waited until the night, after we'd made love and rolled apart, to tell me she was pregnant. She placed my hand on her belly, it was cold with my sweat. She stayed awake clinging to me.

'Listen.'

I said there was nothing, just some wind in the trees.

'Exactly,' she said.

At work Julie ignored me. I stopped her once in a corridor

by the clocking-in machines. Caught her, pressed her. 'Come with me. Just once then, one more time. I promise I won't ask again.'

I phoned her now and then, not out of optimism or resentment, I thought, but to hear her voice. A small thing. If he answered I put the receiver down.

I took to driving out through the evening, car climbing until I'd come across a good view, where I'd stop for a while. Then I'd swoop down to her town, her street, as night fell. Reminded me of my childhood – narrow street, tight terraces, a lit shop on the corner, people loitering. I watched the light behind her curtain, sometimes saw a silhouette.

One time I got out. Bought fags from the shop. I stood to smoke one in the street and looked across to see them coming out. Her man had her by the elbow, as if escorting her against her will. He had a suit on. I took in his profile. He was a big man but with a softish look to his bulk. She looked across with a scowl.

Gail was delayed, but sent down furniture. She came with Mothercare catalogues, baby books, though she hardly showed yet. We went for walks down country lanes. It was full summer, a good one. I chewed grass. She said I was quiet. Was I sure about the baby? I felt I was convalescing.

'Is it lonely here?' she asked.

'No, 's all right.'

It was of course. I'd stopped phoning; my drives out dwindled to one a week, then stopped altogether. At work I avoided looking down at the line, but once I did and Julie was gone, her place taken by a gobby youth.

I went out occasionally, walked into town for a drink. On the way home the lanes were dark, and there seemed to be too much air, but I was sensible enough to leave the car. I was starting to drink more. Other than that I concentrated on work, at night working on my laptop.

I knew I wasn't liked at work, being brought in like that. Round here, Julie told me, you 'worked your way up'. I grew a moustache, realized I was trying to look older. I joined in, gradually, with the office jokes. I picked up their phrases – 'look at them chokkers' – sometimes met colleagues in the social club. I'll give it foive, foive, they'd say to me and finally I knew I was in.

I got on. I worked hard on the final debugging, finished ahead of schedule. Then it was introducing the thing to various groups and individuals. Over and over I made the same speech, pointing to the screen, breaking the ice with a jokey graphic. Went on to the next project, earned more. Gail was pleased.

We were getting on better, she was growing bigger. We sat watching *The Miracle of Life* video. I put my ear to that stretched flesh, listening for movement, heart beat. I never seemed to catch it, just watery digestion sounds. Gail talked about names, clothes, cots and mobiles, even schools but, although I joined in, I couldn't imagine life with a child.

Towards the end of autumn, two days before Gail was due to make the big move south, I was in town looking for a pub. I saw a little yellow poster stuck at an alley entrance. 'J. North Speaks on the Perils of Promiscuity' or some such. A red arrow beneath. There was a little chapel down the alley. The meeting had already started. I tried to peer in through a crack in the curtain. Couldn't see much, the side view of a few townspeople. I recognized a shop assistant from the main supermarket. I crept in the back.

A very large man, with a beard he must have grown since I saw him last, was talking.

'This is what I used to listen to in my youth.' He was holding up an album – *Their Satanic Majesties Request*. He talked of drugs and orgies. I knew him to be lying – drugs yes, orgies no. I could see in his stance, his bulk, the small-town biker Julie had described. Cider-drinking, dope-smoking, him and a few mates roaring through town and out to country pubs by the river on bank holidays.

'Sex and drugs. And that equals AIDS.' He urged parents to look for needlemarks, baggy eyes. His voice was deep, but the accent so soft they could use it in a butter advert.

After came the call for audience members to go forward and of course I went. He held me by the shoulders and spoke straight into my face.

'Have you let Jesus into your heart?'

'Not yet,' I said, 'but I'm interested.'

He showed me some underlined passages in his well-used Bible and said, 'I was sceptical too, at first. I lived life as if I hadn't heard of Jesus.'

He told me about a meeting he attended by accident – someone he met there made him want to believe. You could see he was excited by the prospect of a convert.

We talked, he talked, mentioning 'my wife Julie', until nearly everybody else had gone. We left together, someone locking the door behind us. With his bulk we had to squeeze through the alley's entrance. We walked down the cold street. He talked of the sacrifice of Jesus. We passed the war memorial. I decided I was going to tell him everything. He's probably been waiting to hear it from somebody, I thought.

'Julie, your wife Julie,' I began, 'I know her.'

I went through the complete story from the first time I met her. I was shaking inside, sure my voice was shaking too, but I felt a contentment spread in me.

He gave me quick looks, but kept his head down, kept walking beside me. I was aiming my mouth at his ear, each word deliberate. As I spoke I heard myself saying all this again, under the pressure of Gail's questions, in the future when the mud at the back of the house is landscaped and two kids play on a worn lawn, when there are neighbours, and we are established as the oldest residents. I saw the scene exactly – Gail in a deckchair, mascara running, fists clenched, and I stood in shorts, back roasting, triumphantly spitting the words at her. It seemed as real as the Christian beside me.

We walked the length of the High Street and came to the river.

He gave me a punch in the ribs, but he was already turning away so it didn't hurt. I stopped talking though and watched him lean on the bridge like a tourist gazing at the boats tied along the quay beneath. Towards the other bank, boat free, a nearly round moon was reflected, its nearest edge spreading on the water. I remembered Julie told me he had to be baptized again. Wore a long white garment, swallowed some water. Not enough, Julie said. I wondered if I just got hold of him in the right place, stooped quickly and grasped him just below the knees –

He was mumbling.

'What's that?'

'What you told me – I knew.'

I didn't believe him.

'Shall we go to a pub?' I asked. After telling – confessing, he would call it – I felt two needs, thirsts: one was for a pint, and the other was to hear about Julie, anything really. 'Or is that against your religion?'

He turned from the bridge laughing. The best joke in the world. 'Christ's ministry is everywhere. Don't forget He drank wine.'

'Ar,' I said, mimicking him, ''e did.'

The Optician's Assistant

Paul Williams was father hunting. He came down from his three-street town to the bowl of concrete in the valley. He stood in the street his mother had named, indifferently, at last, the night before. Even with the map he got from the library he had difficulty finding it. He made many wrong turns. He recognized the street from his mother's description – 'I met him at the corner, there's a pub.' He stood opposite the house, number 11. Paper, sticks attacked a low wall and fell at his ankles. The same low wall over there, but the fence above kicked in or blown over and not mended, brambles grown through. One window was boarded up. Mud everywhere – circular splatters up walls, dried out on concrete step and scuffed door. The lawn a few tufts of grass. His ancestral home.

His father – Einstein or Jesus until last night – came out, sniffing the air. Scrubby half beard grey and dark grey and old thick glasses. Off to the pub with his head on one side as if it hurt him.

He had to make sure. He crossed the road and went through the gate tied to its hinge with orange string. He knocked. The wind raised the hair on his plump arms, seemed to fill his throat. Evelyn – another name his mother had given him reluctantly – opened the door. He couldn't focus on her face, there seemed too much of it. He took in orange hair, short and permed, a green blob at each ear. He wanted to shout about the bastard her husband was, but she undoubtedly knew it, since everyone across the valley, up to the hilltop where he lived, everyone in the area knew about the Dales.

'Yes?'

'Mrs Dale?'

'Yes.' Squint.

'Is Ray in?'

'He's up the road. Who wants him?'

'Just a friend.' He stopped. What was he doing here? 'A bit of business. I'll call again.' He turned, wanting to run, and walked to the pub.

He stood by the bar in this completely empty room. He heard the low conversation on the other side of the partition interrupted by shouts, and wondered which voice his father might have. At first he was puzzled by the sounds and strange exclamations, then he worked it out – a card game. Dale came to the bar and leaned over to see if the barman was below, fiddling with the barrels. The trap door was up, a meaty smell of slopped beer, and a small light in the depths. 'Jim-mee boy, you've got a customer.'

Father and son looked at each other, but if Dale recognized anything in Williams he didn't show any sign, his tongue slid up over his teeth, he looked away to the invisible game.

Williams sat and drank, went and got another, sat and drank. He didn't drink much usually, but now he was facing the fact of his life. All through his childhood talking to his mother about spinning molecules and refraction of light, and asking was his father an inventor, a chemist, an expert on the atomic bomb, and she saying no he was dead, or yes he was Frankenstein's monster. All those years spent in the fitting room watching his face fatten and his body change, mirrors giving views from all angles, wondering who he belonged to. Now he could see it – the set of the eyes, eyebrows that ran upward at the end, the little chunk of chin that he had too, beneath the flesh. Signs of Daledom. He was related to the boys who gave him dead legs at school, to the town's only tramp with his moss-cidery smell, to the whole bunch of thieves and layabouts that spread like infestation across the land. Settled gypsies, some said, or coalminers from the Forest who moved in when the mines had shut. A local joke: 'Thar be the Dales.'

Williams lifted his glass, thinking his life would now change but he couldn't see how. Then the door opposite him opened and Angela and her previous walked in.

What caught his attention immediately – her tall, angular frame; then the way her head was held high, flung back really with that nose in front and the dark hair seeming to fan out in the still, beer-dead air. The couple got drinks, huddled in a corner, some under-the-breath argument going on. The man, thickset, dusty, stood over her, finger pointing and finally slamming down his nearly full pint and walking out.

Angela cried. Sobbed, wailed, hit her fists on the table. The barman looked over, went away. Williams had never been alone with a crying woman before, apart from his mother, but she cried to one side, attempting always to hide it. Alarm, tempered with a tenderness he hadn't felt since youth, took hold. When she'd subsided and sat shivering, her arms wrapped round herself, he said across the whole distance of the room, 'Do you want a drink?'

Whilst, and maybe because his father continued to brag and bray next door, ending up in some drinking song of victory, he and Angela became a twosome.

She clung to him for two hours, in a prolonged panic attack. She wanted to bury her head in his chest but it was awkward because she was taller and she rested her head instead against his. She talked so fast and was breathing so strangely he wasn't sure what she was saying. He worried about her friend returning, other people coming into the lounge, his father. Then he felt defiant with the wetness of her cheek on his temple, and he half wanted his dad to walk in.

She became more lucid and talked to him as if he'd known her life intimately: everyone she'd ever met and everything she'd ever felt. He was enthralled and only wished he could see her eyes. He sat there through the time he should be leaving for the last bus.

*

As night fell they walked down endless terraced streets that Williams hadn't known existed. Angela tensed with the cold and began to shout at people and shadows across the streets. They stopped in some kids' playground and he got her to sit on the swing and take deep breaths. Her words, almost visible in moonlit puffs of breath, slowed to a quieter ramble. She talked with the swing rhythm, her feet on her pointed toes like a ballet dancer's, knees high up. He staggered a little in front of her from drink and pride.

They wandered the rest of the night and Angela told him she was mental but not to worry she hadn't been found stabbing anyone yet. She'd been treated badly by men – 'always the wrong 'uns' – but it wasn't that, it was in the family.

'When I was young I knew I was going to be mad, although I knew I wasn't then. I'd go home and my mum had tried to put everything from the kitchen – plates, cutlery, food, the kettle – into the oven. She couldn't fit it all inside so stuff was piled on the open door too. I'd try and put it all back, but soon as I'd taken anything she'd come and grab it. Then one day I came in and started to join her, sticking forks and things in the cracks between the dishes and the pans, and seeing the sense in it.'

They edged back to the town centre, parts Williams knew better, and he told her of coming to the Technical College on day release. He always spent his lunchtimes on a bench by the fountain in the new centre. He told her Prince Charles came to open it officially, and someone had put detergent in the fountain. Charles spoke on the steps of the Golden Egg while elongated wisps of froth floated by. He tried to take her to the scene but couldn't remember his way in the dark.

They ended up in a shelter in the park after climbing railings. 'You can do it,' Angela said, recovered it seemed. They sat with their arms round each other against the cold, under coats. Again it was awkward for Williams – his head at an angle in her armpit, his feet not quite touching the floor. At dawn he pointed out the hill near the top of which he lived. But Angela didn't like to look across such distances, she wouldn't.

'Come on,' she said, 'come and meet my mad mum.'

The next weekend had a flag stuck on it, in his mind. He remembered it so well, most of it. Like so many weekends to follow, it began when the optician's closed at midday on Saturday. He'd hurried his goodbyes even though there was over an hour to spare. 'Off to see your mother?' asked Hugh, his boss, but Williams hadn't spoken to her or seen her in the last week, he'd stayed in his flat.

He waited at the terminus in front of the church with the shoppers and the kids. Alternately he looked for the bus and looked behind him. What he'd miss most, he thought – the rounded brow of the hill framing the tower, the view over the other side – if he went blind. That and some of his customers' eyes.

The single decker with the grumpy driver who gave no change swung round the lanes as if in a groove. Look out cyclist, Williams, sat near the front, said to himself and watched him dismount and cram himself into the hedge. That and seeing Angela, he added to his list.

He'd thought briefly of not going back; she knew his name but not his precise address, he didn't have a phone number to give her. But as the weekend came along the memory of her touch was too strong: her arms clinging, the contact under the coats, her kisses as if she saw in him what no one else did and drew on it.

First there was the room of heat to get through, straight into it off the street. The mother he'd been briefly introduced to the week before sprang up: 'Sit, sit.' He sank into an armchair that bulged in on him, trying not to disappear. A labrador whose hips had gone lay in front of a gas fire, next to it a four-bar electric one burned. He couldn't get used to the mother's intense stare. Her eyes were a kind of light violet and difficult to look at but he had a professional curiosity.

'Are you short sighted?' he asked her, and thought she'd take it as an insult and he'd be in trouble, but luckily she said back: 'My eyes are violet and men come from miles around to look at them, isn't that so, Thomas?' (She addressed the dog.) 'My eyes are landscapes where men go looking and camels get lost. My eyes are an eighth wonder and I've got two.'

Something along those lines. He had perfect answers. 'You're right. Your eyes are one – two – in ten thousand. I should know.' From this night on, Williams came prepared with facts to feed her in the ritual hour when he was almost alone with her, Angela flitting in and out, 'getting ready'. The following week, for example, he tried, 'Half the fibres that convey sensation to the brain come from the optic nerve.' A month later he was saying, 'Joyce, some people claim they can see X-rays.' She was much taken with that.

Angela was off pubs and they tended to go to the pictures,

that first night *Superman 2* because Angela liked the actor even with, or because of, his blue tights. The film he didn't remember so much, he got them mixed up now, they'd seen them all.

Drink making and giggling in the kitchen. 'Mother's in bed by ten,' she said to his worried look. Up, past the first landing and into the roof, to a converted loft, Velux windows showing a starry sky. Then the light was put on to a space full of Angela. Her years of accumulating clothes, records, bric-à-brac, ornaments, jewellery, were crammed all around him, piled high on top of chests and stools, or strewn about the room. Shoes lined up with curled toes and split sides. Books and magazines in stumpy piles. A faded David Cassidy poster. She had all the clothes – platforms and flares – and she willingly got in and out of them for him. She put on a parade for him, her breasts spilling out as she undid her blouse, her knees on display as she tried on boots. Constantly on the move, constantly smoking, ashtrays full of half-consumed ones left to burn down, and sending him for cups of coffee 'to keep us going'. In the early hours she settled close to him, opened herself out like a map and got him to visit all the places.

The pattern became established. Weekends at her place, weeks as before, at work. He started visiting his mother again on early-closing day, taking the customary box of cakes to the sheltered accommodation where she'd landed a job as warden.

'You've forgiven me then,' she said on his first visit to her in a month, 'for going with a Dale?'

It seemed to Williams unforgivable, but he decided not to argue. He didn't tell her he'd seen her ex-boyfriend. There was no mention of it again. Instead there was small talk, mostly Charles and Di whose wedding was all over the papers. As the weeks passed he watched her age before him as if to be in harmony with the residents, and he thought about the stout, heroic woman she had been, at least in his eyes. She came back here alone and pregnant in the early fifties, and defied the hostility she caused, even from her own family who would have nothing more to do with her. Williams remembered the bullies who sometimes chased him to his gate, that song following him – 'Who's your father . . .' His mother came out and stood with her hands on her hips and shouted that they were senseless and stupid and cruel until they went away, impressed by her tenacity. In the house she scolded him for not standing up for himself. But she was to blame for this, overprotecting him, keeping him in, keeping him away from trouble, particularly the local branch of the Dales.

His mother began to notice something of a change in her son. Was his hair combed differently? Was that a new shirt? Eventually she blurted out, 'Is she married or something I never see her?'

It was like an affair. They wrote letters every other week, first him then her, even though they'd seen each other in between. He always cleaned his lenses before he read her squashed up words. Through the dull five days he kept her letters in his inside pocket and served customers – sir'ed and madam'ed and recommended and advised the grateful and the not so alike.

*

Angela, although she could now resist pubs, seemed unable to alter her Saturday-afternoon routine, and he would join her halfway through it, the bus arriving about two. He'd walk down through the shoppers, fountains roaring somewhere, and further down to her patch in the side streets. He'd get involved or not in the series of purchases and sales she made in the row of secondhand shops. She worked in one in the week part time. She had a huge shoulder bag and a strong-handled carrier. She liked to wear her jewellery bargains and would have two or three necklaces looping down and curling on her chest. During the hour-long sit in the café she'd examine the prizes she had come away with, dropping ash on them. She'd read from album covers, magazines, little illustrated books, show him the pictures – elves, trees, rainbows. Trinkets she'd hold up to the window – the room was so nicotine-stained the strip lights were dulled.

Then back along the shops in case she'd missed anything. She knew everyone and would sometimes wander into a corner and have long conversations, leaving him to open and shut dusty books with fine print, or rummage through secondhand jeans for his size, though he rarely bought anything. He saw it as a series of front rooms, he the awkward guest.

One day, clutching a small plastic elephant, she said, 'There. Omigod it's him. Peanut. God, Paul, duck.'

She began a crouching run, in a black skirt that flared out at the knee, her black hair flowing. Williams was so struck by the sight it was a while before he responded and followed, dodging people into the High Street. She pulled him behind a railed in tree. Some of the crowd looked.

'He's coming,' and she ran into the jammed traffic. Williams had to run round, too fat to get through the gaps. Down one street, then another, round a corner. 'Up here,' he heard, and climbed the steps to where she was flattened in a doorway. He tried to stop the noise of his breathing. She was noiseless, occasionally bobbing forward to see if Peanut was coming.

After about fifteen minutes he said, 'Will you tell me about him?' On the steps of these municipal offices she told him more than he wanted to know. She hadn't given up the other men, not entirely. It wasn't serious but sometimes it got her into trouble. Williams felt nauseous, unable to speak, but allowed her to lead him back home, ending up in her bedroom in the afternoon. She waved her mum away as they came through the door, and took him by the hand through the heat.

She sat on the bed and he stood. Her head down. She tried to explain.

'It's just a habit like smoking.' She lit one, shakily, as if to prove the point. 'It doesn't mean I don't like you. The thing is with sex I like it, but it's not important. I won't any more. I'll try not to.'

She leaned forward, her head lying against him. She looked up, she looked in pain. 'I can't have children you see.' She looked away. 'If I could I'd have stacks.'

'Would you?' Williams wouldn't. Who'd want any more of his sort running around?

She fumbled with his flies. Usually he was childishly eager to please her, asking if she wanted this or that application of finger, tongue or penis, and loving his reward. This time he let her do all the work, and felt a surge of power from it. But by early evening he was brooding and couldn't look at her. He told her he was going and didn't know when he'd be back.

The next weekend he didn't go down, nor for several weekends, and Angela stopped writing. He gained weight but there was a tapering off, a dullness. He had long since settled for being an optician's assistant, after his studies came to nothing, but now it seemed unbearable. His vision seemed to dim. He got Hugh to check; funny his boss once more being so close he could feel his Polo-tinted breath on his face. The penlight bending in the aqueous fluid. 'Yes, Paul, stronger lenses needed.' Then came the straight look from his grey-eyed boss, face like a sea creature's, rough and red and open pored – 'Are you OK? Anything I can do?'

He spent three months alone and that time spread either side of his thirtieth birthday. He had a little party at his flat with his mother, Hugh, June the receptionist, and a friend from school he'd recently helped at work. ('I want to look businesslike but not too swottish.') Angela sent a card.

A few weeks later he wrote a letter saying that he would meet her again, if she liked, at the usual place, at the usual time.

'No pull on the ear, no pinch on the nose, glasses you could put on and forget,' he promised Angela who wore contact lenses which she lost or forgot to clean properly. It was a way of getting her to come and visit his town. She could see where he worked, he could show her around. Complete the picture of him: where he'd gone to school; the pond he fell in, going home with his legs covered in green slime; the hill with its view of the five counties, and near the top the rock he'd thought was a crashed meteorite from prehistory.

He didn't want to overburden her however, and thought he'd see what happened. She'd said she wouldn't see his mother – not this time – which he thought a bit unfair as he was meeting hers every week. 'But you get on so,' she said.

Hugh promised to open late on the Saturday just for her. June too would stay to meet her. June and he had spent the quiet times on boring days munching on fruit gums and discussing the best frames for Angela. He showed her a picture. They both thought a black pair, strong frames, quite – but not too – large lenses. 'Do you think she's nice?' he asked. 'She's beautiful,' June said.

It took her four years to make that thirty-five-minute bus trip up the hill. 'But it's a village,' she said after seeing the three main streets on her walk from the stop.

'No, no, a town. It's got an optician's. Piltern's a village three miles along. That's got one shop.'

He introduced her to his colleagues as though they were his parents, and Hugh blinked and blushed deeper on saying hello, but June was immediately talking to her. 'Where did you get that?' and 'Your hair, it's something. I wish,' touching her own crackling perm.

A little stab of jealousy when Hugh got so close to her in the darkened room. He watched as he penlighted her eye, looking so obediently this way, that. He could see a tightening in her body but she smiled at him past the optician. When she tried the lenses he felt again the impact of focus. He'd been diagnosed late and he vividly recalled his own first fitting, here, when Hugh was a young man. The sense of achievement at reading down the Snellen chart; later he could see mud sticking to the hairs of dogs going by, pick out sheep in the fields so far below.

The fitting was delicious. Angela's eyes were so dark an expert couldn't distinguish the iris from the pupil. Posing in his room, she momentarily became the living picture of Sophia Loren, a tad sharper, in a poster Hugh used to have in his window in the sixties. She was redefined. 'Very regal,' he said, 'very very regal.'

She wasn't sure about the hill but was pleased with the new frames which she wore, on his insistence, with no lenses, and let him lead her up past the church where the houses petered out. There were two farmhouses on bends at either side of the road. Over the stile and across the field.

'But there are cows there.' They were all over in a corner but were showing an interest in them.

'Don't worry, just keep moving,' he said. 'The stile's there, look.'

And they were over in plenty of time into the avenue of tightly planted trees, almost a tunnel, and he explained to her it would be like coming out into another world at the end, the quality of air was different, sounds, the sudden view.

He used to wake up and from his window see the hill jammed up close behind the town. At weekends he'd climb here and run through the gap in the trees to see the view explode around him, and then his rock in a hollow below, the size of an elephant and with a gap in it that gave it a trunk. And now he left her and ran it had been so long. A fat man in flight, he didn't know how he remained upright.

He took his glasses off, held them by the stem and all was a racing blur.

'Look – Angel-a,' catching his breath. He saw her coming from the trees her head dropping down and then she pushed her nose into the sky and sniffed and down again. He knew he had made a mistake. He rushed back.

'Paul, Paul, I'm dying.' He tried to put her head on his chest. A column of midges wavered beside them. He led her gently away, back through the tunnel, last year's leaves curled in along the edge of the path. At the other end the cows had gathered, their thick breath changing the air, and he had to take a stick to them, shooing them away, but they were reluctant to move. Angela stood on the other side of the stile in the first stage of panic. When he eventually got her to make her way past them her body seemed as if it was trying to shake free of its clothing.

Back in the lane she seemed slightly better. They passed a farmer – one of his customers, he'd persuaded him to have contacts because his glasses kept falling off with farm work – emptying his car of bags of something. Dogs around his feet.

'Day, Mr Sumner.' He nodded as Angela danced and roared in his grip.

He got her back to his flat and thought he would be able to calm her as he had before on the first night. Now and then it wasn't so bad, she'd lie on him clutching his abdomen, her cheek on his belly. 'You're so good and fat and safe.' 'Less of the fat.'

She acted like a child: the carpet was the ocean and she pulled herself up from it, sopping wet and half drowned, on to the sofa-boat. Then the wooden arms of the cottage suite *would* be oak. Didn't he know demons came out of oakwood, nothing else? Little ones with caps. Why did he buy it? Did he get it deliberately? Useless telling her that this veneer was scratched by him, compass and fingernail, in childhood, his mother's once.

They had sex like a fight on the floor and Angela was braying nonsense all along. It felt somehow there was a third person present who they struggled with.

He thought they could see it out until the morning when he might ring her social worker, whose number Angela had given him ages ago 'for emergencies'. He thought this maybe wasn't going to be one but it turned out it was.

She was hallucinating – the whole side of the building hanging open like a doll's house.

'Are you on drugs?' he asked. She was suddenly lucid: 'That's just it, I'm not. Not taking my medication.'

That explained it. First thing in the morning, even if it was Sunday, he'd ring. But after plunging deep with her into the night he knew he wouldn't last that long. She was quieter but crying constantly and shuddering on the floor, her dress crumpled up on her. At five he said stay there and rushed out of the flat to use the payphone in the street below. He was told to ring for a taxi and take Angela to an address he wrote with a broken biro he found in the booth.

At four on Sunday afternoon at the time Angela should have been returning he was knocking on her mother's door alone. He'd been through a day like no other in his life and seen so many people and at each stage Angela was removed a little more from him. The social worker, still in her white towelling robe, at once took her away. Williams stood waiting in a room so sparsely furnished and tidied that, except for a jumble of books in the corner, it was the opposite of Angela's attic. The social worker came back and spoke to Williams at length. He wasn't sure where Angela was. 'I think the best thing' – he knew what she was going to say – 'would be a short stay at St Thomas. She knows the place, and it's always worked out for the best before. You'll have to sign though, we can't involve the mother.' She drove them over to the hospital and Angela was taken away again for assessment. He waited in the corridor of what was a modern extension built on the back of a Victorian building. Sealed tight in glass and cladding, the air conditioning rattling, he didn't see any patients. He saw lots of doctors and therapists who came out to him at different times saying the same thing – a short stay would enable them to monitor her, the drugs would calm her and give her time to rest and recover. Yet still he hated it when he put his signature to the papers.

All the way on his walk across town he'd been wondering how to tell Joyce, and decided to explain at once. He barely let her close the door before he came out with it.

She went into a gurning act, her violet eyes dying down, her hands clasped into a knot in front of her.

'Will you help me move some furniture?'

Williams had helped with these rearrangements before, there was often some DIY work that he'd tackle, where he'd done none for his own mother, and only the bare essentials for himself. He'd repainted Angela's ceiling what she called a 'friendly' yellow and gone home with his arm aching and his hair and glasses sprinkled with dots of paint. Most recently he'd restored and painted a kennel he'd found in one of Angela's shops, though the near-death dog hardly moved from the rug now.

This time was different. They started off by pushing the furniture in the front room against the window and door, piled it up to create an empty space which they filled with table and chairs from the kitchen, canned food and packets stacked beneath. Williams took the precaution of turning off the fires; she was too busy to notice. Then upstairs to bring her bed down piece by piece, dismantling it with spanners. They moved chests of drawers, bedside tables, emptied wardrobes, Joyce running on some internal engine, while Williams began to huff and puff and stop for rests. They didn't go into Angela's room, it lay across the house above them untouched.

Joyce had left a tunnel through the stacked chairs. She got down on her hands and knees to crawl through. Williams felt an obligation to follow.

In the centre, which she must have planned, there was a space where they both could sit, a little light filtering from the almost blocked window. He banged his head getting in. 'The visual cortex is at the back of the head,' he said. The exhaustion of the last two days finally overwhelmed him and he fell asleep in his crouched position with Joyce awake and staring beside him.

He visited her in hospital. They sat together in the television lounge. There was always the one chair left and she would sit in his lap, entwining her legs around his. She would bend and kiss him quite passionately in front of the assembled. 'Don't mind the loonies,' she said. A man from Australia with a bald head and old NHS glasses stood by them telling his life story from the day he left Australia in 1955. There was something to say about each day. 'As soon as I got here they were on my trail. On August 6th I saw two men across the road with banded hats.' Williams learnt not to interrupt for he would tut tut, say 'Bad manners', and start again.

She was calmed by the drugs but still confused, they said. She did get over-excited at times and tend to jump about in time, as if she were again the long-skirted teenager at discos whom everyone danced with, or rant about someone who stole her cigarettes in 1973. Williams was used to this. She grew friendly with the little community, ate with the nurses, introduced him to some patients – 'This is Karen, she's going out tonight and her husband's coming in. They always take it in turns.' Once he came in and found her along the corridor in a room which said, 'On No Account Enter Alone'. She was inside with a huge Rastafarian, chatting about Haile Selassie. She cheerfully introduced Williams.

When she came out Angela regained her appetite for a social life, to go out pubbing again, the odd dance or party. Williams tagged along miserably at first because he never enjoyed the few discos he'd ended up at, although he liked a drink and didn't mind sitting in a pub. He watched her flit from group to group, discussing, name calling, flirting, and it was hard for him. But then among the regulars he found one or two that shared his interests: one or two would-be boffins. One of them had his own theory of energy that completely baffled Williams though he attempted to follow. The other had a telescope at home and one night brought it along and they set it up in the car park and looked at craters on the moon.

He also found he liked a game of darts, he was good at it. 'It's the belly,' said Angela.

A new phase, one in which he had to share Angela more with others. But she still walked home with him, in summer bare legged, in winter invariably in black tights. The snog in the street for two people well on their way to forty. He looked forward to his night in the single bed which was too small for them both. He always woke to find himself half out of it.

At chucking-out time one night they were in the High Street milling with drinkers reluctant to go home. Williams looked to see the scientist and genius, arm around a brother or a cousin, staggering through the parting crowd. He tried to steer Angela away but she said, 'Thar be the Dales.'

Angela had never asked about his father; he had never asked about hers. Dale was singing 'Moon River' which was his mother's favourite song – she could sing it better. The men held each other and did a waltz as they sang. Angela seemed delighted and for a minute he thought she would join in.

He heard remarks about their dancing skills when the other man fell to his knees and then to the pavement. Laughter. Dale swung about now that his support had gone and Williams saw how old he was in the whiteness and thinness of his hair, like a baby's. His father was overbalancing, and Angela reached out to catch his fall. Williams went forward too and together they helped him to a bench, sat him down. 'There there, you'll be all right now,' said Angela, dabbing at a line of spit on his chin. All the way home Williams' hands and arms relived the burden of his father, prickling and straining of their own accord.

The last customer was a teenage girl, taller than her mother. Williams had never seen a parent and child so unalike. The girl reminded him of Angela, even though she was blonde and blue eyed, a younger Angela that never existed, clear of all worries. The girl wanted contact lenses, the mother was insisting on glasses. 'You don't want to be putting things in your eyes at your age.'

'Try these,' he offered. A feeling of betrayal since they were Angela's frames, and a thrill too.

Sliding the frames over her face, the temples with damp strands, the place behind the ears. Her pupils contracted as she focused in the bright mirror. Her irises solid blue with none of the usual filaments.

'Perhaps not,' he said, hastily taking them off. She was too young for the effect. 'Try these.' He so much wanted to see the scowl flatten out, the smoothness return.

He hurried out to buy extra cakes to take to his mother. She was going to become a resident after all her years as a warden; she'd reached retirement age and had nowhere to go. 'It's fine,' she said, 'I'm only moving next door, and the new warden says I can help her out. She says I'll be invaluable.'

He made tea to go with his gift in the crammed kitchen, so small he hardly had to move to assemble cups, saucers, teapot, plates. 'I see Charles and Di are splitting,' she said while they munched on cream, pastry and jam, but he had more important things to say to her. He told her at last that he had 'met' his father. She was eager to know what he looked like now and nodded as if she expected the news when he told her all he knew.

He also had to prepare her for the visit. 'You'll like her, Mum, I'm sure. Only you mustn't push her, if you see her getting flustered . . .' 'You needn't worry,' she said. She was disappointed she wouldn't have grandchildren. He said she must understand this wasn't a marriage, this was different. As he left he said, 'Don't eat all the cakes.'

There was just time for a quick climb and he started off at the church, a march past the farmhouses and over the stile. He didn't enter the coppice, but looked down where the fields ran in oblong strips of colour right to the outskirts, marked by the industrial estate, of the valley town. He trained his eye hard on the hedged lane that joined the main road at the bottom. He caught a glint: the bus turning off. He followed its progress, guessing when the roof would reappear from beneath trees. In a minute or two he'd run down and meet her at the stop.

Why I'm Late In

This is what I'll say to him: I was getting ready to leave when we heard this shouting and noise. We went to the front window. It was Ian of course. He was screaming at the driver of this car not ten feet from him trying to start up. He was saying: 'Get out, I'll kill you. Come on, I want you.'

The car pulled out. He picked up a couple of just-delivered milk bottles and hurled them. One missed and smashed on the road, the other hit the back windscreen and the glass went white. The car stopped, reversed, the driver had to put his head out. There was a woman, a girl rather, in the passenger seat, couldn't see her face for her hair. Gingery curls, lots of them, skewering the space around her. Like pictures you see in hairdressers' windows.

The man got out of his car. His car was posher than most on the street. He wore driving gloves, dark glasses. He had a full black beard and black glasses, like someone from a spy film. He stood inside the car's open door, looking round at the gathered neighbours.

Everybody who was up was out. We're a nosy bunch on our street. The Rileys, the Khans. Two kids in vests fighting. The woman with all the cats up in her window. We went to the front door too, stood on the step, nodded to the Donaldsons next door. We were in shadow, but opposite the sun was brilliant on them, even so early.

'I'm going to get a fucking knife and kill you.' That shut everybody up a minute. Then Ian went into the house, you could hear him trying to open drawers and Joe trying to stop him. 'Shall I call the police?' Barbara said. 'No, no,' I said, 'it'll come to nothing.'

'Where's the fucking breadknife?' We heard, and the man got back into his car, spoke to the girl – her hair the length of Lorraine's – and drove off.

Making a story of it. While away the time waiting for him to be ready. Hardly ever been up here in all my years. At the beginning to hand in my documents. Now and then a query on my wages. Then this summons this morning. Like being sent to the headmaster. I'll be calm, I'll be steady.

Ian on the streets early, looking in his white socks and hair cut long behind his ears like he should be selling time-shares in Torremolinos. Swaying with the force of the threats that came out of him full pitch. I remember him standing there, selfsame spot, aged ten, while inside his house an argument, one of many. Joe fighting with his wife – Lorraine her name was, nice to say, Lorraine. You should have seen him then – Ian. Barbara remarked on it: permanent worry frown, two little lines on his forehead, like bad businessmen in TV dramas. It was Barbara took an interest in him – 'poor lad' – during and after the split. She picked him up after a fall one day in the street, running out of his house, father gesticulating at the door. Picked him up, patted his head. After that we saw a lot of him. He usually came to the backyard, didn't want to come inside.

Jane had left by then and I suppose the house was too quiet for us. We'd watch from the kitchen as he played alone in our barren garden – a lawn, a yard – ack-ack-acking, his arms machine guns, face tight. Eventually he'd blow himself up.

It was in the backyard that he told us his dream. It was a sign he trusted us. Well, Barbara really, it was her he was telling. Barbara said, 'What do you think you'll be when you leave school?'

'Nothing,' he said quietly. He was a boy always restless even when sitting, but this time he was still. 'I'll be a tramp. I dreamt it.'

'And where will you be a tramp?' asked Barbara and I thought of Charlie Chaplin, but he said nowhere I'll just die in a ditch.

'What ditch?' said Barbara after thinking about it.

'Over the allotments.' Only ditch known to him.

We'd be sat out as late as November, in coats as grey clouds built up. Sometimes you'd hear his father hunting for him, his voice as he passed our entry. The dream he told stuck with me and I've looked across to see if it would be fulfilled. Of course it hasn't because Ian has turned out something worse than a tramp, more reviled – a drug dealer, a house breaker (we're sure he's behind our two burglaries), a cause of violence on the street. Maybe he'll be a tramp later.

I knew, everybody knew, he'd turn out like this. A wastrel – that shows my age – a hoodlum. Barbara thought we could make a difference, thought you could give out better feelings like lumps of bread, but I knew the few hours a week he spent with us would not change a thing. He was someone who needed a spot of shelter, a time away, and we could help there.

The real reason I tolerated him, that I looked forward to having him round, was the fragment of Lorraine that he carried within him, for the light of her that leaked from otherwise dull eyes, for the sceptical angle he held his head as he listened to you. Just like her.

Yes I was I don't know not in love not even obsessed though it may seem so now. I was just happy to have her around. Walking up the same street. That's all. I mean I didn't go out of my way to see her or anything. I didn't plot her movements, spy on her from an upstairs window, which I could have, easily. I just enjoyed the shout of her voice – 'Ian!' – in the street. Nothing musical, although she had a way of saying 'Ock-kay' that slipped like water all through me. Full-throated otherwise. I liked her because there was nothing half hearted about her. She gave as good as she got. Joe – who she had the sense to leave in the end – never touched her but took it out on Ian.

She had a reputation. I tut-tutted with the rest of them,

the street, the neighbours who called round, when it was obvious she was seeing another bloke, or blokes. 'Yes dreadful, Wendy,' I'd say to Barbara's mate from the corner who she goes swimming with. Barbara tells me I'm like an old woman, gossiping, spinning a tale, and it's true. I wish she was more like that, but she's practical: caring, but not fond of the sound of her own voice it seems, keeping it in more than I can. This time I don't agree with the gossips although I know they're accurate. Coming off night shift, smoking a fag I don't want (I only ever smoke when I'm coming home from work, or in pubs), I'd see men drop her off at the end of the street. She'd be snogging, buttoning up as she got out of the car, or holding them off. None of them looked good enough for her. She'd give me a smile as I went past. Something between us she made you feel, but of course all and sundry would be about, and coming with stories to you the next day. 'Yes. Yes,' I'd say, secretly cheering her on. As the lads on the line would say – go for it, Lozza.

After all, with a husband like hers. And what sort of a husband was I, hankering after a near neighbour and her son spending time with us? Well, I never let it show. Nothing but the odd enquiry to those around – 'Does Lorraine know about BT coming to dig up the street?' Even near her, say at the counter of the newsagent's waiting for Mrs Ali to finish on the phone, the *Sunday Sport* and *People* blaring out sex; the top shelf of displayed bodies behind Lorraine's head, close enough to take in her swimming-pool smell, even then I stayed calm, and confined myself to 'Morning,' or 'Hot, what?' She'd show her snaggly teeth in a grin. Sometimes her body would laugh with her. She might snort. I liked it when she showed a bit of cleavage. I followed her out. When she walked, from the back she looked a bit hunchbacky, but her hair, moving smoothly, distracted you from that. In summer I liked to hear the sound her sandal buckles made as she clacked along.

I know how she saw me – an old type, a factory man who spent his Saturdays in the library and walking with his wife down canal towpaths. We lived in two separate worlds parted by a street. Except for Ian who linked us in a silent way, for she never acknowledged that he was with us, and I, curious really when I could have kept her close, had her talk for a while longer, never mentioned his name.

You'd see Ian in those days on the steps of the pedestrian bridge, chipping away with a stone or else kicking a bit of cardboard in the yard of the Hen & Chickens, which I pass every day, waiting for his father to sup up.

He's all right now, Joe is, after a while he stopped drinking, a big achievement, but he started to shrivel too. You notice his parting now. We pass him sometimes, walking his dog down the canal. Never a peep. But then, a period after Lorraine had left, after the news had sunk in, he was vicious. One night Barbara heard sobbing, got up and found Ian in our entry.

I went once to watch him play football. Joe never went, and he told me his school had reached the quarter-final of some local cup. The pitch was misty and I lost sight of him. He seemed to be playing on the far side in both halves. They lost, he was gloomy. He walked home looking just like Joe, with that hint in his pale eyes of his mother. A half-sized fifty-year-old walking the long terraced streets with me.

*

Won't say all that of course. Won't want to hear about Lorraine and all the shenanigans. What's keeping him? See him through the frosted glass. On the phone, shifting about, stood behind his desk. Probably got my file open on there. Date of birth etcetera. Old. Not really, but think, how many summers, good ones like this, have we got left? Five? Seven?

He's coming, head round door. The managerial smile. Doesn't look much older than Ian, but he must be thirty-odd. Whipper-. Up and on my feet. Doff cap. Ha. Into the office. Big high window full of blue sky. He smokes. This is the wrong way round. Stands with the light behind him. Silhouette. Beginning of a gut. Talking on, name, rank and number and

'You got in at 9.10.' Looking at my clock card.

'Aye.'

Wrong way round. I could be his father.

'. . . third time this year. According to regulations . . .'

'Wait a minute. When was that?'

'April 3rd – 8.15; April 15th – 8.17.'

'That was the bus. You check. Everybody was late then.'

'Well third time and you get called for an interview. Nothing to worry about. What about this morning?'

'I got delayed. This boy across the road was creating.'

'Creating?'

'Yes. Shouting, fighting. With this bloke – father of his latest. He got this knife.'

Small screwdriver actually. All he could find. But spy-master had gone so he marched up and down scowling at everybody. I called something. I don't know why. He whirled round, shaded his eyes.

'I got involved. He came over, threatened me.'

As he came over I remembered him do the same four years ago, after Joe had stopped drinking and he'd stopped visiting. Caught me on the way home from here, crossed the narrow street with an envelope in his hand – 'Dad says if you're going up the council can you hand this in?'

'Of course, go ahead, answer the phone.'

Turn away and speak of more important matters. Ian's dream about dying in a ditch – I started to have it, as if he'd given it to me. More and more since Lorraine left, when the street had an after-party feel, stale smelling. Debris everywhere. At night next to Barbara I'd have a gullet of mulched leaves, a watersnake along my spine, a frog for a brain. The thing is, I didn't resist it, I lay there, filling, rotting. At work, here, at my machine, it would take me in, fingers first, and grind, spit me out the other side as gristle for the birds to peck at. Once at home, in the front room. Jane had brought Jonathan with her, we call him the reluctant husband. I held Paul – their two-year-old – while he pummelled my lap as he tried to climb up. Jane was celebrating, although she was nursing a cold, brought a bottle of wine round, because she'd passed her test. Jonathan sits there as glum as I've seen him. The jutting chin the shape of a baby's shovel. While Paul scrabbles at my ears with those little perfect nails his father goes off to the bay window and proceeds to solve a puzzle off the back of a matchbox. Matches laid out across the table. I look at Jane to see if there's anything in her face but I can see she's got used to it, like rainy weather. That's when it happened. Blossom was blowing past the window and I was tasting mud. Actual grains, clods of dirt on my tongue and teeth. I had to put the baby down, cough.

'Apologies, apologies. You were saying?'
    'This kid across the road. Came over. Threatened me.'
Behind him as he came across I could see Joe apologizing to neighbours for their loss of milk and offering to pay. 'Your father's calling you,' I said. He smiled. 'Calling me what?' I wanted to ask him where Lorraine lived, if he knew. Not that I'd do anything about it, just be happier to know what streets she walked down. Look it up in the *A-Z*. Maybe just one trip over, bus or train, to see the local landmarks. To fix it in my head.
    'Was that it? He threatened you. Anything else?'
    'Yes, he knifed me. Cut a nostril. No, inside, you can't see it much now. A scratch. He pushed me down.'
'Lost your tongue?' Ian sneered. He glowered down at me with his mother's eyes and said, 'Perv. Fucking perv.' All the street was listening in. I thought, they've heard worse. Barbara shouted for Joe to come and get him. From the floor I watched them walk back, the two heads bursting into sunlight and the rest. Ian shrugging off his father.
    'I hurt me back. I had to get the blood stopped.'
Mike from next door and Barbara helped me up. 'You'd better sit down,' she said, 'take the day off.' I shook my head but let them sit me down. Mike stood in the room awkwardly, his three-year-old clasping his knee and staring at me. Her first bloody nose? Barbara said she'd make tea but instead went to the window to view the still noisy scene outside. 'One day,' she said, 'we'll have to get the police on him.'

'Yes, OK. That's fine. Fine.'

Should have phoned in sick as Barbara said. Could be out now in this blue day combing the city for a sign.

'I can go?'

'You can go.'

I can go.

Cheer Up Lucky Lips Forever

When I was young the sky was mine. I was always getting close to it – up trees, on roofs, the iron bridge. I loved hill-tops, exhausted from the climb, lying looking up into the blue. I'd been on a plane once, to Spain – and back – saw cirrus drift above tiny mountains and woods running on for miles. I was sure I could fly, just jump in a certain way and off I'd float, skim houses and see faces I knew looking up at me.

The Iron Bridge: we'd perch on its stanchions being big, as a train whooshed, dulum, dulum, faces at the windows, on its way. Its steps were the scene of our games, fox and hounds, double dare. Chic Goloskov threw lighted ping-pong balls and vinegar-hardened conkers from the top when our gang split in two. Bunt jumped from the bridge into a coal truck in the sidings, climbed out just in time, as the rattling started. Jumping as it picked up speed, he did his knee in and was all covered in coal dust. We argued where he would have ended up – 'Crewe.' 'No, Swindon.'

Sometimes the driver of a diesel, bored by waiting in the sidings, might let us up to see the engine. At his signal we'd slip through the silver fence and scramble up the gravel to the raised line. A climb past wheels bigger than me, having to be picked up to see through the cabin window. The men's *Daily Mirror* and sandwich box amongst the levers and notices – EMERGENCY . . . TOOLS . . . And, 'Take them on a tour, Andy.' Like *Voyage to the Bottom of the Sea*, machines slotted together into a display of dials, levers and buttons, behind wire mesh. We slipped in our pumps moving down the oily corridor, eyes and nose deep in the sight and slick smell. And ears: humming, clicking and sighing or rushing like a storm so you couldn't hear what was said.

'Not enough women,' Double-B (Bob Banks) says after the first couple of lectures. I agree: too many suits at this conference. It would mean too much drinking, too much smoking and me just taken it up again. It would mean standing with our backs to the bar, swilling some local ale, saying we were going to go across and ask that one, the one in the skirt; after all we were free agents, well-divorced the both of us. So it proves.

BB repeats his observation as we board the train home in a northern town I'd not recognize again, except by a curious gassy smell that seemed to linger in car parks and lobbies. He goes on to lament the waste of time – 'company time, my time, your time' – it had all been. What is it about conversation with your slight superior that exhausts you? I nod at him as we slide into seats that say 'sleep' to me. Through the stickered window I see the station and the clutch of high-rise around it disappear into the fog.

The hitch to my dream childhood was a girl we called the Blob, who lived close to the Iron Bridge in one of a set of three railway cottages, right next to the line. She'd taken to following us at a distance, calling over her fence at us. She apparently loved me. She called me 'dah-ling'. On walks home from school when we'd taunted and spat and ges- tured at her she would call she lo-o-o-ved me, Teddy, Teddy. (She thought I looked like a teddy bear.) She'd lunge at me. Playing football, sometimes I'd twist up for a header and see her by the corner flag cheering. Sitting at the back of the class, she'd sigh when I came in and then take to muttering to herself like her grandmother down the shops. 'How come her brother's got a different last name?' asked Chic, whose own last name we all stumbled over but thought fabulous.

The Blob – mud hair, webbed feet, lice feeder. An adult and a baby at once, big but blubbery. She still had some- thing, like babies have corners of blankets, that she fing- ered when nervous. Something small she took out of her cardigan pocket. She was known by this yellowish cardi- gan, worn throughout the year. We all claimed to have seen fleas jump from her tangled string hair. It was death to touch her. And she loved me.

The teacher made us do the surface-tension experiment together, the one with the bowl of water and a pin. She didn't understand the idea of a skin on the water. She sat so close our knees touched and layer after layer of smells settled deep into my pores.

'Look, boys, I'm scrubbing my hands, it's all right,' I said to them in the bogs later but they still avoided contact for a couple of days.

Once when she called to us over her fence and we shouted back, her big scary brother 'Prof' (because he smelt like a chemistry set) came up behind her. Just his face, thin, raw, and his red tufts of hair were enough. Before he could speak we were gone, into the bushes.

I think we go through Sheffield, Derby, somewhere, towers of lights smudged over the window by fog and condensation. Half hearing Double-B's theory of women, what they want. Carriage warmth, train roll had me.

BB, shaking me: 'I don't believe it,' sounding like Victor Meldrew, 'first they divert us, and now we're stopping.' He peers over me: 'In the middle of nowhere.'

I look out; we've pulled up under a bridge. The light dimly lights the word 'CHIC' on the metal side of it. The last C is bodged at the bottom so it could be a G. I remember him doing that. He hung from one hand, one foot wedged under the bridge railing, grinning back at me, and pretending to jerk and fall.

On the other side of the line from Blob was a pasture field with a herd of cows always in one corner or another. Also a coppice, a brook only full in winter, a scummy pond whose ice Brenda Martin fell through. Alongside that was a hillocky, grassy area we called the flats. Here we'd meet and share out what we'd scrounged or nicked fom home: a slab of chocolate, some flat pop, matches to make a fire and cook up insect stew. Afterwards we'd piss the fire out to hear that hiss.

An older group of boys sometimes met there. They were very particular who they talked to but they didn't seem to mind me, and I'd lounge near by as they squatted in one of the dips in the grassland. A magazine; a pack of cards; roll-ups galore and a Zippo lighter; a green bottle of cider they all swigged from.

'Girls' bums.' Scarred John Trentfield educated me about sex. 'That's what grown men look at. Tits are out, it's bums now. Arses.'

Blob already had tits.

He showed me a shiny picture of a woman bending over, looking back over her shoulder. I wanted a closer look. 'You're too young.' He picked at the long scab on his cheek. He said it was done in a knife fight.

Derek, older than me but not their age, appeared over the top of the knoll, in brand new Leeds kit and unmud-died football. 'Doyouwanna joue au football avec moi?'

'Fuck off.'

'Focken cunt.'

'You know that hut?' Johnnie Scarface said. 'Where they keep the salt? They put the man from the crash in there, one leg off, dying and bleeding. They thought the salt would save him, *stalk* the blood, but he died in there. And, Derek, that's where you're going.'

Twenty years ago seems to be lying outside the window, the same herd out there looming at the fence. Beeb's

dissertation continues, the word woman or women punc-
tuating. I tell him I'm going to the toilet, but I turn the
wrong way. The passengers are stirring, impatience in
some voices. They turn, mobile phones stuck to their faces,
to see if I am a guard coming to fix the problem. I'm bent
to look through the smudged windows at my piece of land
and the sky I flew in. Suddenly the noise and vibration of
the train ceases, a defeat called to the fog outside. I expect
to see the two ghosts from the crash come to the window,
but they don't.

The crash – two dead, forty-two injured, it said in next
day's paper. We were coming out of primary school when
it happened. A noise we felt in our knees and teeth. We
wanted to see but teachers ran out and stopped us. Miss
Crouch still had her glasses nestled in her hair. Soon there
was blocked traffic, police. Nobody had thought of the Iron
Bridge and three of us slipped out through the churchyard,
ducking past the cold cave entrance, and circled round that
field. Once through the hedge we raced across, crushing
buttercups and trying to ignore the cows – one was a bull
surely – starting towards us. I stabbed my foot straight into
fresh cow dung, spraying up my leg. But then we could see
it all and we were up our bridge in no time.

There below us as we knelt on the rim, holding the still
cold bar on this hot day, was a carriage spilled right into
Blob's back garden, joined to others hanging off the line. I
thought of a necklace, a throat twisting. The people lying
on their sides, upside down, ties, handbags in faces, clutching luggage racks to scramble free. Already there were
winches being assembled, men in uniforms, and doors

being cut through, sparks and thin lines of smoke.

For two days we couldn't get near it, although the trains started running again pretty soon. Then Chic hit on the idea of using my 'in-floo-unce' with Blob. Get us into the scene itself.

We waited until we were sure she was on her own (spying from the bridge). I asked if we could look for our lost ball (we'd kicked it over just before).

The yard looked like it had been smashed up and was being put back together. Bent pipes and gravelly rubble, makeshift fencing, official yellow tape still stuck to things. I saw the remnants of Prof's motorbike, some bits of engine. Chic and Bunt searched, I had to keep Blob occupied while avoiding her hands. Hands the size of my dad's. One thing, though: she had eyes the shape and darkness of Emma Peel's, if not the quickness and sparkle.

They found a shoe, ripped along one side and a spot of red on it. We ran over the flats and put it inside the hole we'd discovered and enlarged beneath overhanging grass, with our other special things.

Miraculously, at the end of the carriage, the triumvirate of youths who looked like they were camped there move on, pushing each other and singing 'Ooh-Ah, Can-to-na.' I'm left with room to pull down the window and lean out into the cold and gaze through the broken fence opposite to Blob's plot. A light in the kitchen, a wobbly crayon-yellow square, but the house is tucked up in fog.

I think about getting off, going over to check the details. I can hear a car changing down in the lane beyond, the treacherous corner where I came off my bike. Bunt and Chic could still be here, over in the hidden houses watching television with wives from our class maybe – Bunt with Jackie G, the one with the sly smile and abundant curls. But I seem to remember hearing that Chic had emigrated – Australia, or was it America? But most of all I want to know if Blob is still there.

One Sunday when all the gang seem to be caught up in family visits I go by myself to our patch of land. I lie in a willow, arm dropping, watching my fingers sway in the space above the grass. The air is full of traces – buttercup, cow dung, dampness trees give off even in the heat, smell of trains gone by. I tell myself I'll go soon, *The Avengers* is on.

She comes in through the kissing gate muttering fast as usual. Her mouth is a minor spitty squall. The grass dimples in her wake. She won't see me, too rapt, I can idle on.

And yet when she has gone by, almost out of sight, I say experimentally, not loudly, 'Bubble Blubber Blob', and she stops, looks back. I swing down, a small moment hung from the branch still in the air before I touch down.

'Je joue au football?' I ask her.

I take her over the flats, building on my talk in her backyard. She plays with her comforter. I see it is round and gold, or brass. A little bell without a pea. She also has three fluff-covered Love Hearts which she asks me to read.

'Cheer Up, Lucky Lips, Forever.'

'Teddy, you make me shwoon,' she says. I think.

I say, 'Take your pants off then.' We're in the dip, invisible to everyone except from the bridge, behind her I know there is a hollow with a shoe, a one-hundred-beater marble and crumpled pictures of women.

'No, that's dirty.'
'It's not, it's love.'
''Snot.'
'What's love then?'
'It's hugs and kishes.'
'And it's bumsh. Take your clothes off.'
'Only if you kish me.'
'All right.'
'Go on then.' A terrible pucker.
'Clothes first.'

Her underwear is grey and her skin the colour of old glue left in pots, hair already sprouting under arms, and even some down there, a little. She tries to undress without showing anything. A train rumbles into the station.

'Focken cunt. Turn round and bend over.'

'You love me now, Teddy?'

My eyes seem to sting as if from swimming-pool chlorine in my effort to focus there, there and there.

'We'll get married, Teddy.'

'Turn round and stop calling me Teddy.'

I go and stand close. I press my trousers against her. A feeling as when I begin to fly, that special ankle twist that releases me upwards.

'Leachie! There you are. Thought you'd fallen on the line. God, take a look at that.' BB lets the girl hear as she squeezes past. His hands squeeze air behind her back.

Even after her brother beat her, scraping cheek skin off her with his fingernails, even though I'd still curl my pretty lip in rejection, Blob came to me when I was alone and asked to meet again. Prof had seen us from the bridge as I zipped up and left, but, strangely, he left me alone. I still dodged through garages and crouched amongst flowers when I saw him coming.

Her garden across the track where once dead people lay. She must still live there, I can see it, children of her own. A life maybe better than mine; it's possible.

The train begins its domino rattle, engaging each carriage. 'Thank God for that,' says BB. 'Perhaps we'll get home tonight. Shut that effing window, it's freezing. Come on, the bar's open.'

I close up the window and watch twenty years being dragged out of me, faster and faster as the train gathers speed.

Previous Lives

I'll tell you what first struck me. It wasn't your eyes, that was to come later when I got close enough to see the gold flecks in them. No, it was an earring, slice of silver against your neck catching the sun in our kitchen one day. I'd just got in from school, still in stupid trousers and tie, and you and Carol were giggling, passing a joint back and forth. Carol was 'wowing' everything and you, laughing, passed the joint to me. Told me how I was to smoke it: to let some air in and hold it in my lungs. 'No, no,' you said and showed me, put your chin in the air, your head back and the earring was revealed. Don't know why but my eyes were fixed – you and Carol continued chatting and laughing, drinking coffee after coffee, while I tried to stop staring. The rest of your face, the small gap between your front teeth, a pinkening complexion, the curled mass of brown hair halfway down your back, these details accumulated around that tiny scythe, scything the air beneath the lobe.

Sitting up here in my bedroom, knees either side of a corner of my sister's old and scratched dressing table, the mirror reflecting a faded picture of League Champions Villa (remember that!) and a grimy window full of rooftop and cloud, I imagine you behind me, sat half out of bed, watching my back. Your clothes scattered across the room. Your smell instead of long dead semen and old socks. Your fingers reaching . . . The scene's as bright as a cornflakes ad, and I turn to nibble at your cheek like a fish against glass.

All day we used to stay up here if we could, even if the sun was blazing, as it often did that summer. Used to lie in your proximity feeling alight, listening to the muffled sounds of the M5, the Sikhs chatting outside the Gurdwara at the bottom of our street, the bloke opposite always tinkering with his car.

If we couldn't be here we'd be down the park, the one surrounded by towerblocks, Bowie's 'Let's Dance' on everybody's radio. In the November before you left we saw a fireworks display there, my nose in your smoky hair. The high-rise residents getting a free look, framed heads lit by bursting colours, fire's orange tearing at the night below them.

Those days when I was smeared with you, hands, face, everything. Knew those days were numbered, knew it from the start, wasn't surprised at the final serious chat, you sat on the bed staring at your bare thighs, curtains tight behind you. I looked down too, letting each word make perfect sense in my head.

There goes Dad coughing up in the sink – 'He's showing off,' you used to say, and I always think of that now – his ability with phlegm improves. About all that does. See him in his vest, a dying man, and only fifty-six.

How sweet he was to you, stumbling on his words, always liked you. I'm sure he knew you stayed with me although you were supposed to be in Carol's room. Perhaps he was past caring.

On his way back now is Dad, on his way back to the television, which he watches from Anne Diamond to the National Anthem. 'What time is it?' I ask him and he says, 'Four minutes to *Bullseye*.'

Wait, he's lingering outside, does that, I can hear him breathe, noisily as ever, wants me to have a can with him. Without Mum, without Carol, without work, he's a bit lost. He still reads the Situations Vacant but they're all for VDU operators ('Is that some kind of medical scan?' he asked me) or some mysterious thing called 'Tele-sales'.

Reckoning back, I've always thought I was conceived after England's World Cup victory (I'm named after Peters); Dad impregnating Mum in a bout of football-inspired euphoria. Since then, according to him, football's gone downhill and life has followed. Each year of my life is worse than the last, bringing only new problems, difficulties to adjust to. Mum, for instance, had her first 'mild' stroke in 1970, and in '73 Dad was made redundant for the first time and had to take a lesser paid job. 'When I was your age,' he begins and I get out quick because I don't want to hear about Harold Macmillan ('our greatest prime minister'), National Service and immigrant-free streets again.

After Mum died what he was mostly was puzzled, like everybody in the world was asking him difficult questions. But he's finding his voice now, and it's different from the kindly rasp you knew. This afternoon, for instance, he was on about the dustmen who haven't been for two weeks because of Easter. They never did that in his day. He then compared other services to the past, and got on – as I knew he would – to pre-decimal prices. 'What do you want me to do about it?' I asked him before escaping up here.

Only the box keeps him quiet, and that's maybe worse. Last time he rented one he let the man persuade him to get a remote. He showed it to me flat in his palm like gangsters weigh guns in cop shows. 'Look at them, all them buttons.' And he explained each button's function, words copied from the salesman. Ads, news, bullets, laughter in quick succession. For weeks every night was like that, Dad sat in the chair that knows his knotty, lanky shape so well, aiming the remote between his knees, mishmash of sound reaching me upstairs writing to you. Yes, I've been writing to you for weeks.

A smoke in the morning sets you up. Got some oil from Don, smoke that while I listen to Joy Division (the cassette you made for me).

This stuff's expensive though – glue's cheaper. Did you know I used to sniff it? Made the hours go quickly. You'd start at say ten in the morning and before you knew it was 16.20 on your friend's video and his mum was due home.

Used to hang about mostly with this kid from school – gone skinhead now. 'Bulldog' he likes to be known as, but I call him the Prat. Big mates we were until we had this wrangle over a girl, and . . . but I won't go into that, let's just say that when I fart it's in his direction. The two of us would go down the canal to those disused factories (Dad used to work in one), and squat amidst the broken glass and mangled steel bagging it.

Funny sensation, not unlike this stuff, but tighter, colder somehow, at times I'd hallucinate. Once we'd been bagging for a while and I looked across at him smiling and shivering vaguely, realizing I must look like him but I felt entirely separate, alone. I wandered through the abandoned machinery that had nettles and lupins growing through the rusted holes in the metal. I climbed over the rubble and up some slippery wooden steps into a room where I met people.

A massive family, innumerable people were there, greeting me as if I'd just returned from some long, perilous journey. One or two had tongues like typewriter keys, others had eyes that slipped out of their sockets and swung as they talked. It seemed they had adopted me as a kind of mascot and prepared a tea for me – silver cutlery, tiny sandwiches, candelabrum, the works, like a scene from those Sunday night Agatha Christie films. The talk switched to something like French which I instantly understood (and you know how bad I am at languages), a girl stood beside my chair, had her tongue practically in my ear as she whispered love words and began to unbutton my shirt. But my arm came off with it, painlessly. All around, in twos and threes, people stood up, undressed, and flexed their muscles showily before removing arms and legs. As if part of a solemn ritual, they piled them on the table. Then I heard matey below and realized I was in an empty room, an ex-office, and I watched him below trying to tip over an old lathe, grunting and swearing at it.

That was one of the better times; one of the worst was when we were over in Sandwell Valley, a load of us on push-bikes on that pedestrian motorway bridge, bagging it and our talk full of swearing bravado and heroics. Glue made the cars below zooming streaks. Slots opened in the sky – 'God delivering letters' I said but the rain was spearing the Prat. His chest heaving in his T-shirt, he really did look like that bulldog, you know all pectorals and no waist standing on its hind legs. Started to threaten us, didn't he, daring us to take him on, he'd throw us one by one into the arrowed colours below – it was too neat for him, he wanted to see it messed up. The rain and the glue stung and goaded him. The trouble between us was just starting and it was definitely me he wanted to check whether the traffic was keeping its distance.

. . . can't concentrate any more, the cassette's finished, downstairs Dad's put on the 'Morning Romance' film, and next door's kids seem to be demolishing the place from the inside, like the ones in that story I read for O-level.

Carol's fine by the way, as well as can . . . no she's not, she married Don, you said she would, so how can she be? We both called him a bearded fool – remember that day he was going on about Pink Floyd's vision of madness? He'd half disappeared into his hi-fi then and now there's little of him left.

Sat with Carol sipping half lagers in the Taj Mahal waiting for our takeaways, she tells me she is 'going with' a married man, holds my hand tight while she admits this. 'I suddenly got envy,' she says. 'Well not suddenly, I don't know, I'd drag Don out for an evening and all the other couples in the pub look happier, they actually talk to each other. You know?' I knew. Leave him, I say.

But of course it's not as simple as that, it never is. The other bloke's got a family he's reluctant to leave and of course there's the baby, my nephew. Know about him? David they call him and I suppose I should say what a lovely thing he is but he just seems to cry when I'm about. Once I held him in my lap and he started. I looked about helpless for help, Carol was in the kitchen talking to Dad, and Don, after asking about you – 'Seen Jean lately?' with a smirk – sat back on the sofa smugly stoned. The creature cried and writhed with increasing power, as if I was apply-ing torture, and I felt as pathetic as its father, smiling vaguely at us from across the room.

But I still go over there, she's moved out Frankley way, that fifties council estate on the edge of the city. Can't keep away really since Don's always got some (it's a 'safe house' for dealers) and I've rarely got any money. Went over yes-terday in fact, had smoked the last of the oil and was rest-less, Dad getting on my nerves because he couldn't get his bony body comfortable either, he seemed particularly morbid.

So I turn up on her doorstep and she's there thin as Dad but even taller, in inevitable dungarees and scarf, looking down at me, baby straddling her hip. She's tightened up since you last saw her – like her skin's drying out. 'All right Mart?' she asks but doesn't stop to natter, knows what I want and leads me to them, Don and his friends passing the bong around and moving their heads in time. I get in the queue too; brother-in-law Donald, looking like a hijack victim in his second week, nods at me (about all he can manage). I like the thrill of the smoke putting down roots in my lungs and blossoming in my brain. Your fault, you put the hunger for it in me.

One of them, I'll call him Ratsy after Dustin Hoffman in *Midnight Cowboy* (remember that night?), wants to do the bucket trick, because of my entrance I think – wants to see if I'm up to it. Well, I was game. Someone fetched a red bucket half full of slopping water. Don produced the sawn off plastic bottle from a cupboard, and we gathered like Red Indians round a camp fire. Ratsy, watching keenly, lit me the first blow. Soon thick streams of smoke were exhaled from mouths and nostrils and lazily filled the already murky room. The talk of when Bob was so stoned he got his verticals and horizontals mixed and couldn't get up, and of how Pete swallowed half an ounce of Leb in a police car – 'what a night he had in the cell' – faded out and the music, Marianne Faithfull's 'Broken English', took over. One by one they got red-eyed and serene. I'm as bad, going back for more and crashing back to the floor of this room that started to spin like the Rotor and me hanging on non-chalantly, thinking of you. Something about being stoned in this house brings you closer, can feel your touch as if the intervening years had dissolved. Maybe it's Carol's presence – sat now at the corner of my vision as if presiding over the fallen bodies. The baby in her lap looking like a flesh question mark to me.

When I leave this merry bunch I'm surprised to be in daylight (or grey light, this being April). The sprawling estate seems more than ever cubes stuck in the countryside, tacked on to the city. I wait for the bus with the day-patients from the psychiatric hospital, a group of low buildings set in greenery opposite. One, a tall Afro-Caribbean in a crumpled white suit and Woolworth sports shoes, puts his thumb up to everyone and says 'Hello bug-gar'; another jolly-looking bald man with a white mous-tache as if he'd Tippexed his upper lip (badly) laughs high like a schoolgirl when he says it.

The bus, when it comes, is two decks of madness with workers progressively crowding it cracking jokes, this being Friday. In my state I can't cope and get out and walk. Head down and don't stop. You can imagine my squat thighs, so different to Dad's, pumping: you always said I walked too fast. Streets go by. I cut through the burglary belt where tulips are reflected in the hub caps of shiny cars and then into the narrower streets of Bearwood. Each window, inches from my face, has the news starting up. Thought about call-ing at your house but what would I say to your family? 'Hello, you don't know me but I used to sleep with your daughter before she got that job in London.'

End up in that park, my head full of space I wanted you to fill. I reacquaint myself with the green, scrawny piece of land: football field all mud, hut's paint hidden by the same old graffiti, the scrubland round the sour pond where we embraced.

But as I was settling on one of our benches, evening falling and lights going on in the towerblocks, I saw Prat and his gang. Heard them first before they became silhou-ettes approaching. I slipped quickly into the bushes, unsure whether they'd seen me.

They charge to the swings, boots hitting concrete. Prat gets centre swing and proceeds to boast about his part in Villa Youth's rout of City fans. His talk's full of 'rucks' and 'wasting' people – the gang grouped round chip in with their own exploits.

I'm cowering, waiting to sneak away. The wind starts up as sudden as a car crash through the trees. You're there somehow, a flame tottering in the air, merging with the dots of drained colour about me, the slyly lit greens and greys shimmering. I'm stoned remember – so stoned I make a lot of noise scrambling out through the railings. 'Who's there?' I hear and they charge into the shrubbery. Prat recognizes me as I run up the street. 'It's that bastard Turner – I'll get you, hippy!' I'm insulted – me, a hippy. But they don't bother to give chase, all I get is a pebble in the back, winds me a bit.

Dad's been calling me for the last hour. *Grandstand*'s on and he keeps shouting up, 'Come and see this, Martin, it's really something,' or 'They've just said the Villa are winning.' (A very momentous occasion these days.) I feel obliged to go down after last night. I'll go through the results with him like we used to, years back. I'll even check his coupon for him.

We got four draws.

Last night I get in, my back hurting a bit from the pebble, to find him gone maudlin on me. Cans are lined up at his feet with the folded newspaper which says: 'REINCARNATION – Top Stars Tell of Their Previous Lives.' *Wogan*'s just finishing and he's pretending to watch it. 'Where you been?' he asks without looking up. I sigh. 'Nowhere.' He turns and grasps my arm as I go past, looks up at me, eyes opaque with drink and emotion, his breath coming up from bad lungs. He's trying to say something but all he can manage is, 'You don't know the half of it.' 'The half of what?' I say, irritated. 'I'm serious,' he says, coughs. 'Your mother and me, we got on. Really well. Didn't argue, not much.' Not quite what I remember but I nod him on, wait for more. Nothing.

'Shall I get us some tea?'

I'm glad to escape to the kitchen; the dope wearing off, I'm tired, my limbs ragged as parsley and my throat silted up. While I put on the pie and beans next door's cat is on our bog roof agonizing into the clogged ventilator. The magnified howls fill the kitchen until I chase it away.

As we eat from trays in our laps I notice how my actions copy his, arms up together to shovel pie, and the way our stomachs respond in unison. Our heads simmering with the after-effects of different drugs. Behind the screen, in that box, the action is loud and fast, but the room is fuzzed by fag smoke and the fumes from the faulty gas fire.

After we've drunk and smoked he again turns to me, leaning out of his chair, examining me as if he'd never seen me before, his eyes more in focus now.

'Was twenty-five years ago today we married,' he says.

I realize he's seeing her in me since I'm that side of the family, short and dark and with her eyes.

He leans further out, muttering something, and suddenly I want to tell him about you, about the gang in the park, about Carol's botched escape attempts. Then I notice a smear across his cheek and something about the bean juice against the white bristles prevents me from speaking.

*

Poking through the cupboards for scraps of you, I come across the two or three boxed games abandoned there since Mum had her major stroke. The tattered corner of the Monopoly set . . . boys versus girls we used to play, they usually won.

You only knew us when she was in hospital waiting to die, a shambles of a family we were then, in disarray. It wasn't always that way. I recall a time, I must have been twelve, Carol fifteen (you sixteen!), when we had dinner out the back one hot July Sunday. Dad, as ever a stickler for convention, had complained that we ought to have a proper Sunday dinner but the combined assault of Mum and Carol overcame him. We only get two hours of sun before the terrace at right angles cuts us off, and we didn't want to waste it indoors. The three of us sat in a line on a patterned blanket that filled our patch of lawn, Dad sat on a kitchen chair with his *News of the World*. Mum wore a mauve nylon top and it wasn't long before her shoulders got red and her one streak of grey hair – something to do with her stroke – glittered like liquid, as if her skull had sprung a leak. We faced the sun, and behind our backs were the remains of food, chicken legs, Sunblest crusts (Carol still doesn't eat them), Coke-furred glasses. Mum had bought a honeycomb, and I chewed the sweet wax. Between the shadows of my bare legs the swards of grass were as bright as plastic. Mum hummed to a Beatles song being played on the *Jimmy Saville Show* two or three doors down. My sister had her older arm round me trying to grab the bee's nest but the elusive taste was mine.

I had, as far as I can remember, my first 'proper' erection

then and it must have been soon after that Dad came into my room clutching a copy of *Woman's Own*. ''Spect you get it all at school these days, Martin, but in case you don't, read that,' and he put the magazine on my bed. It was open at 'What to Tell Your Child about Sex' – something like that and probably by Claire Rayner. He stood by the door a minute, thumbing the handle. He reached deep for some parental advice. Finally, quietly, he said, 'Sex, now, can be a good thing – beautiful,' a word I'd only heard him apply to Villa strikers or a factory job, 'but it's not everything.'

Sometimes it takes me a long time to get here, to pick up a pen and write to you again. I circle and circle it, forget it, go out, do the shopping (a new Tesco's opened in the precinct). Lately my head's full of that Talking Heads song 'Burning Down the House' – annoying, I don't even like it.

But finally, weeks later, here I am writing to you. This being June, the sky's the colour of used water in our rattly twin-tub and the rain comes down and down. Is it raining in London?

All right I'll get to the point. Carol's told me. I knew something was up when her first sentence after 'All right, Mart?' was 'Things change, you can't expect everything to stay the same to suit you.' She's definitely leaving Don, had enough. Says she was talking to him about David's future and he was so stoned he fell off his chair. So she's off with the 'other man', taking David. And they're leaving the city, going to some small town in the East Midlands where his sister lives – want to start afresh. Don't we all. But you probably know all that, because she has a second piece of news for me. She prefaces this with 'You've got to face up to reality' and 'Rip up that letter you're writing. Jean isn't like the one in your head, that's a dream Jean.' 'How do you know?' I ask. 'Because I've seen her.'

Apparently you come home quite regularly, pop over to see her. Apparently you're getting married.

Send us a picture so I can burn out his eyes.

What I can't stand, and it's really stupid, illogical, but what I really can't bear is the thought of that softening look, your whole face changing in someone else's embrace. It takes a bit of getting used to, this news, it won't leave me, like someone whispering in my ear from the minute I wake up until I go to sleep again. Even then you're always in some corner of my dreams leaving the imprint of your kisses on some featureless man.

When you have an inquisitive man in your house, sniffing out your secrets. Dapper Brummie with thin moustache and matching tie, large smooth nose with no bend, bulb or blemish. A shining example. He was from the DHSS checking our claims. 'And you've spent your redundancy money, Mr Turner?' Into each room he went with his clipboard. 'And who sleeps here?' (You did once.) 'Sister left has she?' Wanted to know everything, gleaming eyes ready to burst with discovery, but didn't want to know about the letter from the Gas Board I showed him (the one that quotes the Fourth Schedule to the Gas Act, 1972, which we all know and love), didn't want to know about that. Sort of man who'd never had an insight in his life, looked like an extra in those old Joan Collins films they're digging up now. I stabbed him in the just-big-enough-for-two hall as I unlocked the door on to our thin sloping street, I stabbed him just behind his large clean earlobe, in my mind.

Stabbing mood lately. Went for a job in the city, put a tie on, haircut, and after the interview the boss calls me in for a 'personal chat'. Said I was close to employment if only I changed my 'negative attitude'. 'Now's the time to be sensible and sane,' he said. Behind his head was the city, crane and towerblock, his jaw was dark and massive working against the sky. His handshake went on for many hours. 'Why don't we get down on our knees and worship work,' I said; he soon let me go.

Well today's the day I reckon. I was just looking out the bedroom window at our always busy street – the Asian kids with brilliant jumpers tied round their waists playing cricket, the bloke across the road fixing a radio into his car (same bloke, different car) – when this 'powder blue' Escort pulls up. Carol's head emerges, her white parting like a thermometer. She's downstairs now in hushed conference with Dad over coffees in the kitchen. David, for once, playing the mouse.

I'm sorry about all that above, I've no right. I did write a lot worse – pages and pages of abuse laced with pleas – as the day of your wedding neared. But I've calmed down now.

So congratulations then. Be happy.

Have you still got those white trousers? We used to walk close, not holding hands or anything, but close enough for your hips to knock mine now and then. From the park up the slope of this road, calling in for tobacco and papers at the corner shop.

Carol's calling . . .

*

Take care of him, she says! Look out for him, she says.
What does she think I've been doing these last couple of
years? Who does the shopping, the cooking, the cleaning,
argues the toss with the SS? Dad can't cope with them – if
they told him he had to shave his head to get a furniture
grant he'd believe them.

He's visibly shaking when I get down. 'Give David a
kiss,' says Carol. He shakes his head – 'That's it then, is it?'
– puts his hands on his hips to steady himself.

The two of them so alike looking at each other, two sets
of dark brown eyes, two sets of small ('nibbly' I used to call
them when young) teeth, two minds wondering how to
break apart with grace. Should have just disappeared,
Carol, I'm thinking, should have just gone.

A two-note horn sounds. 'That's him. I said to come
back in half hour to give me some time with you. D'you
want to meet him?' 'Married, you say?' 'Uh-uh.' 'No, then.'
Clever, Carol, clever, got him to look away. 'Well we'll call
round some time.' She turns to me, pecks my forehead,
squeezes me, lifts David. The creature is smiling, very rare,
seems interested in what is going on. 'Ta-ra a bit then,
Mart.' 'Yeh, see you.' At the door, in sunlight, she has her
heart-to-heart about Dad.

I watch her go to the car and strap David in the back
seat, her slim haunches tight as she leans over the folded
passenger seat. Her partner is obscured by her but I see his
hand, fat rings on fat fingers, tap her rump. Across the
road the amateur mechanic takes an interest, wiping his
hands, his naked belly-folds smeared with oil, as he gazes
over. As they move off, Carol waving like the Queen, he

resumes work on the radio and several blasts of 'Spirit in the Sky' play out their exit.

Next time you walk into a supermarket take a good sniff. That thin, cloying, fish-like smell near the tobacco kiosk – probably the air conditioning lowering some chemical that makes you salivate as you come in. That smell gets in your hair, clothes, sticks to your fingers.

Next time you see me in Tesco's, come in. Yes, that was me, a bloke almost in a brown nylon overall and name lapel. You had a good look, didn't you? Calvin, this black lad I work with, came up to me kneeling over a box of canned soup in the aisle. 'Hey your luck's in. There's a real smart brown-head staring through the window at you.' I was up like a shot, but only in time to see you and your mum disappearing. Nearly rushed out to greet you, pricing gun in hand, when I saw your hair – short and spiky now, then. And long, obvious, 'clangy' earrings. Moment I saw this, clocked your walk, I realized that was that. I lost my desire instantly. Strange. Bye bye Jean, I said to myself, with only a little regret.

'Smoothness of transition,' he says, 'that's what I want,' and proceeds to tell me how he will achieve it. He's a short balding man with pointed grey sideburns and fierce blue eyes, about Dad's age. He stands in the I'm-a-good-bloke-but-no-nonsense stance, steady, unflinching, hands in pockets draw up his jacket. I nod at his plans, trying to avoid Calvin's silent insinuations with eye and tongue that I am arse-licking.

We get on, me and Calvin, skive in the store below,

gorging ourselves on Yorkies, laughing at boss and shoppers, Calvin producing joints from all over his person.

What with work and everything I haven't had much chance to write, haven't been up here – apart from to sleep – for weeks. Winter's coming on now – me, Calvin and Dad are going to the fireworks display next Saturday.

Carol's fine, as far as I can tell. She's written, says she may be pregnant again. Says she'll be down for Christmas and we'll meet John, and Dad's agreed (we composed a letter together in reply) – secretly he's looking forward to it, keeps saying we ought to get this and that. With me working he thinks there's money for everything now.

One last thing you may be interested in, since I mentioned him, Prat and his pals beat me up. Well, not exactly. It was one night in September, me and Calvin sat on the steps outside our house, smoking, chatting. They came down the street, over the brow. Four of them, snide comments as they approach. Before I could stop him Calvin asks them to speak up. And round they get in a semi-circle, threatening. 'Got yourself a new friend then, Turner,' Prat says, 'not good enough for you, are we?' etcetera, etcetera. Can see he's been on the glue or maybe just pissed. As I get up to go in he pushes me, Calvin threatens him, he fists me. And guess what, Dad comes out. Breathless, skin-and-bone Dad. 'Clear off,' he says like the doorman in the comic I read when I was a kid. 'Go on, move. Making a ruckus on my doorstep.' Perhaps because there are now three of us (bullies count odds), perhaps some sudden reverence for age (unlikely) strikes them, but Prat's mates take hold of him (he's still snarling) and make off down the street.

'You're bleeding,' Dad says when we get in, and looks for a tissue.

'I'll get over it,' I say, tasting the blood.

A Man

Once I was driving and I couldn't believe my eyes. I went past, eyes up to the mirror, foot off the pedal. Yes, there they were, four of them. No more than kids.

I'd just been to my girlfriend's, Joyce that is, but hadn't been able to do much because her teenaged son, Russell, had stayed in.

All night I'd sat there, him on one side and her on the other of that big sagging sofa where we'd first made love. They argued over me. Not about me, or not that you'd notice, but across me. He wouldn't eat, hadn't eaten.

'Make yourself something,' she said.

'Don't want anything,' he said, misery itself.

'We got beans, eggs.'

'Not hungry.' He was wincing, face down.

'Sausage and mash, then. We've got packet stuff.'

'Nothing.'

She went through a whole list of stuff.

'Leave him,' I said and he glared up at me, his eyes one band of blue hate. I had this boil thing below my ear and it started to throb.

I was annoyed anyway that night because I wanted a long talk with Joyce, something I'd had to work myself up to, and when I got there I couldn't, not with Russell there. I was going to tell her it was over between us. I'd been seeing this other woman, Brenda, someone I'd met in a pub. (We'd had a few torrid nights and now I had a toothbrush there.)

It was 3rd January, end of the holiday, and it was back to work in the morning, back to normal. I'd used Christmas as an excuse to Brenda, saying I couldn't spoil it for Joyce, so she made me promise to tell her that night. 'And make it plain,' she'd said, 'tell her straight.' I was supposed to go back to Bren's and spend the night with her, and go to work from her place.

So when Russell went upstairs I thought I'd take the chance and tell her quickly, all in a rush before he came back, but it was Joyce who turned to me.

'Can't you talk to him?' she asked.

I just frowned at her, my mind on other things.

'He's been sniffing. He'll be doing it now. He's addicted.'

'Sniffing? Glue, you mean?' She'd not told me this before, but he was the type.

'Lighter fuel. It's worse. I come home of a evening and he's slumped here, and the room's half full of it, like fog. And the smell – he could blow himself up. I have to open all the windows and then I can't rouse him.'

She tried to squeeze my hand for reassurance but I withdrew it.

'Can't you have a word with him?' She was blinking a lot, which she does when she's nervous. I thought I didn't want to see those watery blue eyes again. I thought I wouldn't miss them.

'What good can I do?'

'You're a man. He might listen to you.'

'Huh,' I said, 'fat chance.'

And now on my way home after achieving nothing, after promising Brenda I would, thinking of her waiting up for me, fat and warm in the nightie I bought her, rehearsing the 'I'm sorry but . . .' speech I would make, now, when I least needed it, this.

I was on that raised road between Birmingham and Dudley, lonely at this time of a Sunday night. I'd just emerged from the close dark jumble of factories and warehouses and was out in the open with the city's lights spread out as far as you could see when I spotted them under a streetlight.

Could feel my stomach turn ever so slightly.

Absolute silence, no cries, no laughing. I wound my window down to make sure. Night went into me. Then one voice, two, urgent, whispered, as they pulled him down the street.

I'd stopped, waiting, wondering what to do. Another car behind slowed, but passed, the passenger looking back – the face a small, dim white blur.

The boy they were carrying, dragging, was naked. White, thin, blood or mud all up one side. I heard his hip scrape the pavement. One of them noticed me, but didn't bother, didn't do anything. They turned on to a street running down between a housing estate and a playing field and disappeared.

I sat for a bit thinking, then turned the key, but let the engine stall. Everything seemed clear outside, a frost settling over Birmingham. Cold got into my fingers and the boil began to gnaw at my neck. Then I started the car again and this time drove away. I headed home.

Dad, Mum, Paula and Tom

I suppose the worst you could have said about Dad in those pre-Major, pre-Paula, Thatcherite days was he played the Beatles loudly. If he joined in the chorus of 'I'm a Loser' you had to watch out, it meant some bad time at work, some frustration. 'Drive My Car' he played only in summer. His list of Great Women was topped by John's Aunt Mimi, included the mid-sixties Jane Asher 'for inspiring Paul's greatest stuff', and even extended to Barbara Bach for being such a good drinking companion for Ringo.

'Where do I come in all this?' Mum would ask, and he'd say she was in a Top Ten of her own. She wasn't convinced. She said he ranked the day he saw John Lennon in New York above the day he met her a few months later. 'How could you think such a thing?' he'd say with a grin.

But Mum has her obsession too – computers. I thought it was just a phase, I remember when she disapproved: 'a distraction from books'. But her job as a librarian demanded she use them more and more and soon she was talking about drives, modems and remote databases. Now it's multimedia and the Net. She scolds me for not wanting to get e-mailing (I've stuck with books). When Tom got an Atari she said, 'I don't like the look of that,' but within a few months she was beating him at the game that came with it. His boasting got to her – I'd come down in the morning to find her in her dressing gown, long legs tucked under her, hunched over the screen, 'Take that you bastard.' It took a while, but in the end she gave Tom a damn good whacking.

I was pleased about that. You're supposed to look up to your older brother. Not me. I admit I used to think his Zep albums were great – they made Dad wince. I coveted the leather jacket with the elaborately stitched Guns N Roses emblem – an early version, the guns blue and old fashioned, like muskets. I used to look at the girls posing in his motorbike magazines. Dad used to watch from the window as Tom in his leathers pushed his pedal bike up the suburban road, and call for Mum to have a look. 'Don't be mean,' she'd say, but I could see his point. I grew out of my heavy metal phase before I reached my teens.

So we went along happily the four of us until Tom did get a motorbike and caused some real trouble. The police became regular visitors to our 'little house in Harborne' (Dad says, though it's more Bearwood). First it was speeding; then a fight; a stolen car; drugs. If they hadn't been for a month Dad would be saying, 'It's a record.'

Mum thought there must be some strategy for dealing with him. She took out psychology books from her library. She tried kindness and punishment turn and turn about. Alternately she would say to me, 'Talk to your brother,' and 'Ignore him. He's a dickhead.'

He was on the verge of being sent down, doing community work, when he met Paula. The first we knew of it he was moving into her flat in Balsall Heath. 'Who is this girl?' Mum asked. 'Can't you bring her round?' But he didn't, not until the weekend after he told us she was pregnant.

Although she's scruffy – rat-tailly hair trying for the white Rasta look, layers of ethnic clothes – Paula's very different from Tom's other girlfriends. (For some reason he's never had any trouble attracting women; maybe it's the long curly hair, maybe the one-minute belch he can sustain after a bellyfull, maybe the smudge of oil always on his cheek.) She's pretty, but you have to look hard to see it. Her head hangs forward from rounded shoulders, a slightly hooked nose that catches the light. It was the smile I liked – a little mouth curled up at the corners (Tom's curves down to the same degree). She has a lemony smell which I thought was her until I smelt it later on a girlfriend (perfume) during a bus stop date. What made her really different was her liveliness. Unlike her predecessors who could just manage a grunt to an offer of coffee, Paula more than held her own, in fact often led the family banter.

In the course of a few weeks Paula changed us all. Mum, who had always stated that babyhood was a disease she was glad we'd got over and had not held a baby since if she could help it, now started giving advice about birth positions, analgesics. She wanted to touch the belly, a small football then, and Paula said, 'Put your ear to it.' She got the family albums out for the ritual 'Tommy and Stevie shots' but didn't zip through. She lingered and explained the constant vigilance Tom needed when I was born – he kept scaling drainpipes and running off. 'He still needs it,' said Paula and she and Mum were friends.

Dad suddenly became semi-vegetarian and a radical. 'I only like a bit of bacon is all,' and nodding on her plans to unseat Mrs Thatcher. 'The poll tax will kill her off you see.' Not bad for a middle manager who recently went out for a steak (Mum and Dad's twentieth wedding anniversary).

What clinched it for Dad was she liked the Beatles. He called her 'Polythene Pam', and she responded, 'Why, do I look like a man?' She wasn't a fan, she hadn't stood in Menlove Avenue like Dad, but she knew the main stories and would mull over Stuart Sutcliffe and Pete Best with him. Dad talked to her about the day he saw Lennon coming out of Central Park – 'On his own, walking ahead of me.' He told her he would have stayed in New York – he'd gone for a trial period for the parent company – but couldn't take it, he'd got vertigo up on the thirty-sixth floor. He'd never told me about that before.

She even made Mum and Dad laugh about Tom, telling a tale of when he invited an off-duty policeman back to the flat for a smoke. They liked the way Tom was beginning to change. Picture this: Tom washing up; Tom proudly discussing the merits of names as his girlfriend bloomed so that she could no longer squeeze into the space between the table and the wall and had to swap seats with Dad. She still rode pillion though. A week before the birth there were two helmets on the side as we sat around eating crisps and drinking wine, Dad saying yes he would march against the poll tax, Mum saying she might, and Tom outside tinkering with his bike, singing Motorhead's 'The Ace of Spades, the Ace of Spades'.

In the end it was just me who went on the march with Paula, Mum and Dad scared off by the riots in London the month before. Tom had more important things to do like attempting a wheelie down the old railway track. Paula was contemptuous – she had to pay Tom's tax as the earner. We started near the front of the march with the bongos. All the way from Chamberlain Square, through New Street (this was before it was pedestrianized), I carried four-month-old Lisa, her toothless mouth wetting the shoulder of my jacket. Paula pushed the pushchair with the red 'Smash the Poll Tax' balloon tied to the handle. Lisa enjoyed all the people and noise, the police dogs lining the route. By the time we'd swung round the Rotunda we'd fallen behind the rest because we had to keep stopping to wrap and unwrap her in the changeable weather. Lisa was attempting something – 'AA-gee,' after the 'Maggie Maggie Maggie Out Out Out' chant.

It was me, and Tom occasionally, who did a lot of the feeding and changing during Lisa's first year – learnt the exact tilt of the bottle she liked. Mum, Dad and Paula seemed always engaged in political debate. Apparently Dad had done his bit – he was there in Grosvenor Square (he must have been all of seventeen), apparently he'd spread peace and leaflets through Birmingham. Mum, too, with her first-hand experience of deteriorating public services, claimed to be left of Tony Benn.

From the resignation of Howe to the downfall of Thatcher the excitement built in our house. Dad came home from work and flicked the news on to find out the latest. The night Thatcher shoved the BBC man out of the way in Paris we all went across to Paula's, stopping for cans of lager, and stormed the Balti on her corner.

I was coming down the slippery steps of the backstreet club we'd all met in, a sharpness of vinegar in the air from the fish shop that backed on to the small car park. Lisa was two plus, Major was in, we were depressed. I was still going to the meetings but now that they were desultory, bickering and ill attended, I started leaving early. That night I came out after twenty minutes; it was raining softly and the car roofs were rilled with rain. There was little light to speak of, just a glow from the city above the houses and light only falling from the windows where the gang were debating. I was wondering where Paula had got to when I saw her. A corner of her dress backing out of some hole in the wall, somewhere they stashed the dustbins, a corner of multi-drainpipes and clogged drain and nicked into the building like a wound. She was backing out, and I would have called but saw she was pulling her dress together at the front, buttoning those red triangular buttons, and thought Tom again, a quick one before he shoots off down the pub. Maybe this always happened, which was why, perhaps, Paula seemed so distracted at meetings lately. But it wasn't Tom who tumbled out, missed his footing and crashed into her, it was Dad.

When later that night I see him, I run after him and catch

him on the street, catch his shoulder and spin him round. A man fat with guilt, his cheeks like sides of beef in the raw air, the air going in and out of him at a speed to shake him. His newly long hair (despite the bald patch) dampened and curling behind his ears. Those stupid glasses he's just bought steaming up. The hands out like Jesus, only they look like blocks of wood coming to life. I'm jabbing at him with my finger – What sort of person are you? What sort of person? – and a couple of people have gathered to watch, a bus load of passengers staring down at us by the time I let fly with a gob rolled to the tip of my tongue. 'You leave him alone!' 'I'll phone the police.' They think I'm assaulting him – young man: mugger. I didn't know I could hit but my fist lands on his ear and he's trying to push me off as we fall, and then he squirms away from underneath me.

Lisa is four. She says things like 'Trees with flowers on are girl trees.' She sings 'Yellow Submarine'. She makes up stories. I play with her plastic gorilla, King Kong to her Lucy Locket. Paula and Mum disapprove of Lucy, but Lisa loves her and combs her hair. Mum has now initiated her into the graphics package, and her coloured in print-offs adorn the kitchen wall. She's forgotten Tom, she's forgotten her grandad.

When I see him, at meetings he rings up and arranges, I always think he should slink in furtively. I should be sardonic. It should be a dark, shadowy place, jazz playing. Instead it's Littlewoods basement café, and a muzak version of 'Yesterday'. After the 'How's your mother and what's she up to?' (plenty – she's started her MA), and the long stares intended to express contrition, he tries to find out if Tom knows yet. Does he fear a beating up? But Tom doesn't know, we'd all know if he did. He's gone off with his gang, sleeping on a couch in an Erdington flat last I heard. Then he says, 'Do you think Mum'll have me back?'

I always shake my head. Mum listened to his confession the night I bruised him. He tried to explain it all away as a reaction to getting demoted at work – he hadn't said but it made him feel less of a man. 'I should say less than that, younger than Steve I'd say. Nine? Come back when you're forty-four again.' They agreed never to tell Tom, and called me in, still bristling and ready to punch, and got me to promise too. Then she said, 'I've changed my mind. Don't come back at all.'

What I can't tell him is the unlikeliest thing has happened: Paula's started to make return visits to our house. Not just dropping off Lisa for Mum to mind on her afternoon off – I used to act as intermediary so they wouldn't have to talk to each other – but now staying, and a tentative version of their original friendship is emerging, based on doing what's best for Lisa. Paula sits in her old place in the kitchen, and laughter, long gone from there, is beginning to return.

Mum really has turned vegetarian (animal liberation has replaced talk of socialism), and with the righteousness of a convert won't even let meat into the house. I eat my sausages with Dad. There's little left of the man who ten years earlier danced me round the living room to 'Twist and Shout'. He looks like he's fallen out with himself, the balding speeded up, even some acne. He's lost his job; he's nearly fifty. He looks at me and I give him forgiveness, grudgingly but it's there, but it's not what he wants, he wants a way back.

I was with Helen, a girl I'd been pursuing over a couple of terms, who had finally consented to go out with me just as I was about to go off to university in Manchester. Up close though I'd been disappointed, her skin tight like she'd already had a face lift, and the glorious ringlets that first attracted me were growing out. We were getting fish and chips before I realized where we were, and while she was ripping a small hole in the paper I steered her down the side street and pushed her into the niche. It was still light and I looked up to see the city blocks jut up into the pale sky. Then I went at her. Bins clattered. She held her chips in front of her, they were getting squashed. She was saying, 'Hold on, hold on.' All around this spot was a forcefield marked by dropped chips. Her slippery mouth was under mine, her body half bent back. But I stopped, and shuffled back, and stood while she was grounded and uncertain, legs at angles. 'What's the fuckin' matter with you, Steve? I'm covered in chips.'

Mouth
Stories from Tindal Street

**SHORTLISTED FOR THE ARTS COUNCIL'S
RAYMOND WILLIAMS PRIZE, 1997**

'A roaring start in the shape of Gaynor Arnold's "Mouth", a chilling first person account of being young, female and vulnerable in the supposedly cotton wool and dayglo worlds of family and boyfriends . . . particularly effective are Alan Beard, Alan Mahar and Godfrey Featherstone, whose close-cropped Brummie monologue is about the most successful use I've yet seen of our notoriously difficult local dialect in fiction. With smooth and well-crafted tales set in Chile (Penny Rendall), Calcutta (Annie Murray), Yemen (Mike Ramsden) and amongst Pakistanis in South Wales (Barbara Holland), the book gels well around issues of race and identity . . . As the key to both our city's rich diversity and its status as a potential trigger for anarchy, the explorations are timely and wise'

What's On

'Outstanding quality . . . as compulsive for the reader as a box of expensive chocolates for the chocoholic . . . each story occupies the heart long after the work is put down'

Raw Edge Magazine

'Godfrey Featherstone's wonderful extravaganza . . . Alan Mahar's "Spoken Urdu" is brilliantly observed . . . the uncertainty of sex and the chasm between generations, and the heady clash of cultures that make up the modern city'

William Palmer, *Stand*

Mouth: Stories from Tindal Street
Tindal Street Fiction Group   ISBN: 0 9528246 0 4   £4.95

Available by mail order from:
TSFG, c/o 32 Frederick Road, Birmingham B15 1JN.
Please enclose a cheque for £5.75 per copy (incl. p+p)
payable to Tindal Street Fiction Group.
Telephone enquiries to 0121–449 9702.